M000189096

He took two steps across the room and gathered her in his arms.

"Don't," begged Delphine. "Please don't."

He slid one hand up under her hair and put the other firmly in the small of her back and pressed her tightly against the length of his body.

She could feel a slow, rhythmic pulsating from his body, beating on her own. She told herself she should break away before he kissed her. But it was already too late....

THE
FRENCH
AFFAIR

MARION
CHESNEY

FAWCETT GOLD MEDAL • NEW YORK

For my friend,
Mary Ann Bachman,
with love.

THE FRENCH AFFAIR

Chapter One

✣

Lady Charteris gazed on her countrymen with wide, curious eyes. They were the first French people she had seen since she had come to England at the age of six, seventeen years ago, when Sir George Charteris had rescued her—the last of the noble house of de Fleuris—from the horrors of the French Revolution.

Since her arrival in England, she had lived at Sir George's home, Marsham Manor in Bedfordshire, where she had been brought up by her kindly rescuer. On her eighteenth birthday, Sir George, then forty years of age, had proposed to her, and she had accepted, finding marriage a gentle continuation of the calm, sheltered life she had always known under his protection. Lady Charteris had never spoken French, except with her tutor, and had never considered France her home.

But when news of a fair being held in Cavendish Square to raise money for the French *émigrés* who had flocked to London in the thousands to escape the Terror was announced in the morning papers, Delphine, Lady Charteris, had been overcome with a desire to go, despite the protestations of Sir George's sister, Mrs. Bencastle, a grim widow of uncertain years.

Sir George had died three years ago, and Mrs. Bencastle seemed to think that Delphine was sullying her late husband's memory by this visit.

"You are English now," Mrs. Bencastle had grumbled in the carriage on the road to London. "I never could see what George was about, to risk life and limb rescuing those Frenchies from the guillotine. Untrustworthy, that's what they are."

Delphine had simply compressed her lips and refrained from replying. She had found long ago that it was best not to enter into any argument with Mrs. Bencastle but simply to go ahead and do what she wanted.

Mrs. Bencastle had made her home with Sir George and Delphine after the death of her husband ten years ago. After the death of her brother, Sir George, she had appointed herself as counselor and companion to Delphine, a situation Delphine bore with the calm patience she bore everything else, from bad harvests to the disapproval of the local county who still considered her a foreigner and also damned her as a "lady farmer," since she saw to the management of her estates herself.

It was late September. Cavendish Square was full of noise and color. A small sun rode above the smoky pall which always shrouded London, and there was an exhilarating nip in the air.

Although the French *émigrés* had been in London for over two decades, it was still socially fashionable to support them by giving balls and concerts and fairs such as the one Delphine was attending.

The *émigrés* who had managed to smuggle out enough wealth to maintain a good position had set up a sort of Faubourg St. Honoré around and in Manchester Square. Those less fortunate huddled in the hundreds in squalid lodgings in St. Pancras, and the ones who made their living by using their wits inhabited Soho. Gently born men and women with no training in earning a livelihood made a gallant shift at self-support by using the accomplishments of happier days. Many became teachers of French, of music, of fencing, of drawing, and of dancing. Some found homes as tutors or governesses, others as dancing masters.

One nobleman set up as a tailor; another stooped to shoemaking; a countess opened a shop for the sale of ices and other dainties; an accomplished gourmet exercised his skill as a salad-dresser for parties. Some faithful servants set up restaurants and kept their old masters on the proceeds. Young people were trained to make artificial flowers and straw hats.

Why the *émigrés* continued to be loved by society was a mystery to the Mrs. Bencastles of England. The war with France was finally over and that ogre Napoleon was incarcerated on Elba, but their soldiers had taken so many British lives. The poorest of the French *émigrés* took their superiority to the English for granted. Most never bothered to master the English language. They plumed themselves as missionaries of dress, deportment, taste, and elegance, despising their host John Bull, who "lived on spleen and tea."

And so, to Mrs. Bencastle, Cavendish Square was thronged with posturing popinjays. But Delphine found herself caught up in the frivolous atmosphere, the intoxicating gaiety. She moved among the booths with their fluttering ribbons, listening to the chatter and rattle of rapid French all about her.

She shyly asked the price of a fan in halting French, and then shook her head in amusement at the exorbitant sum. The pert *demoiselle* behind the counter promptly mentioned a lower price. Delphine again shook her head. The price went down again, and before she knew it, Delphine found herself haggling away in fluent French while Mrs. Bencastle stood a little apart, glaring in disdain.

Mrs. Bencastle looked, in fact, like a female John Bull. She had a heavy, pugnacious face and a large stomach and bosom formed into one round mass by an Apollo corset. She wore a low-crowned hat, very like a man's, its severity modified by two tall pheasant's tail feathers stuck in the band. She was dressed from head to foot in black. She wore, winter and summer, wool on top and flannel underneath. Delphine found that the only reassuring thing about Mrs. Bencastle was that she was always the same—grumpy and critical. There were no wild swings of mood, and Delphine could not once remember having seen Mrs. Bencastle smile.

Mrs. Bencastle held her large umbrella firmly by its heavy ivory handle, which was carved in the shape of a dyspeptic duck, and wondered how soon she could get Delphine to leave. Delphine, she thought sourly, was turning more French by the minute.

Delphine, despite her English upbringing, was French in appearance and manner. She was small and energetic with golden skin and masses of dark hair. Her eyes were large and pansy brown and slightly almond-shaped. She threw back her head and laughed at something the young salesgirl was saying, and Mrs. Bencastle thought bitterly that even her laughter sounded French. Of course, George must have been in his dotage to marry a penniless foreigner hardly out of the schoolroom. Poor George, thought Mrs. Bencastle, heaving a gusty sigh. Little did he think as he lay on his deathbed that his young wife would be laughing in that sickeningly carefree way when he was hardly cold in his grave. The fact that Sir George had died three years ago meant little to Mrs. Bencastle, who had gone into mourning for her own husband and had never come out of it—as far as dress was concerned.

Sir George had once told Delphine that his sister

had always been so, that even as a young girl Maria had perpetually looked as if she were prepared to attend a funeral.

At last Delphine purchased the fan and joined Mrs. Bencastle. "Have you seen enough?" asked Mrs. Bencastle crossly.

"Oh, no," said Delphine. "I really must buy some more things to help these poor people."

"These 'poor people,' as you call them," snorted Maria Bencastle, "would go farther and fare better if they learned the king's English. Throwing my brother's good money to a lot of wastrels..."

Delphine stopped walking. "Enough," she said in a small, cold voice. "It is because I manage the estates so well and study the latest improvements in agriculture that we have no wants. Sir George left us comfortably enough, but I have trebled his money as even you must admit, Maria. Furthermore, if you are going to persist in being rude and ungracious and in spoiling my day, then we *will* return to Marsham, and once there, we will discuss your future. You do not need to stay with me, Maria, as well you know. I am prepared to set you up comfortably anywhere you wish."

"I only said what I thought was right," mumbled Mrs. Bencastle.

"Then if saying the *right* thing means being rude, why do you not essay to say the *wrong* thing once in while," said Delphine tartly. "You're a bore, Maria."

And with that, she twirled her parasol over her shoulder and began to make her way through the crowd.

Mrs. Bencastle stood stock-still and stared after her. Never in her whole life had anyone dared to call Mrs. Bencastle a bore. She was outraged. The local county did not call on Delphine, Lady Charteris, and without her, Maria, where would Delphine be? Mrs. Bencastle conveniently forgot about her gossiping to the local county behind Delphine's back, about her exaggeration of Delphine's "Frenchness," about her own surly temper, which had caused the county to cease calling.

She stalked after Delphine to give that young lady a piece of her mind, forgetting it was very hard for anyone to lecture Delphine. She simply stopped listening.

Today was the first day Delphine had ever shown any signs of temper. Which all came about, thought Maria, from the pernicious influence of all these foreigners.

The very *smells* seemed foreign to Maria Bencastle's British nostrils, a combination of musk and perfume and garlic and wine.

She spotted Delphine quite easily. No other lady was wearing a bonnet quite so frivolous or quite so *pink*. She was standing at the edge of a crowd, craning her neck to see what they were looking at. Maria took up a bulldog stance at Delphine's elbow.

The crowd swayed and parted, and Delphine quickly nipped through the gap to the front. Maria, not to be outdone, elbowed her way after her.

Delphine, aware of her presence, bit her lip. Maria was tolerable in Marsham Manor in the heart of Bedfordshire, even with her constant grumbling. In the country, Delphine found she hardly noticed this constant rumbling grumble of complaint. But here, among this cosmopolitan crowd, Maria suddenly seemed as welcome as a ball and chain.

Shrugging the irritation away, Delphine turned her attention to the performer who was attracting such a large crowd.

He was an extremely tall, very good-looking man in a rakish, devil-may-care way. Delphine thought he looked English. He was wearing morning dress: blue swallowtail coat with silver buttons, buff breeches, and Hessian boots. His gold hair shone in the pale sunlight, and his eyes were as blue as the country sky.

He seemed, in all, too elegant a creature to be performing at a fair. He was juggling six silver balls with quite amazing dexterity, his long, white fingers nimbly catching them and spinning them around until they seemed to move in a circle of their own volition.

Then he stopped and made a magnificent bow. A tiny urchin with a face of ageless evil, dressed in the shabby livery of a tiger, promptly started passing 'round the hat. Delphine fumbled in her reticule for a sixpence. Then she noticed that the elbows of the well-pressed morning coat were shiny with wear and that there was a patch at the heel of one of the performer's boots.

She pulled out a sovereign instead and threw it into the hat.

"Got a yellow boy, guv," shouted the tiger to his master. "Flash mort over here." His voice was pure cockney.

The performer looked across quickly. Delphine tried to escape, but the crowd behind her was too thick.

The performer walked towards her and looked down into her eyes. "Thank you, fair lady," he said in a lazy, sleepy voice. "But a look from your beautiful eyes is worth more to me than all the gold in London." Delphine stared up at him, unable to drag her eyes away.

He raised her gloved hand and kissed it while Mrs. Bencastle snorted, "Mountebank!" and the crowd cheered.

His voice was English and cultured, carrying the polite, lazy damn-you-to-hell accents of the English ruling class.

Already regretting her generosity, Delphine snatched her hand away and gave a stiff nod. He made her a low bow and went back into the circle formed by the crowd where he began to balance a plate on top of a thin pole on his chin.

Delphine turned away, anxious to be gone.

She did not know him, and yet... and yet she was *disappointed* in him. That an Englishman of such obvious breeding should make such a *clown* of himself.

Delphine felt unaccountably depressed. A small wisp of cloud covered the sun. Mrs. Bencastle was mumbling away about the disgrace of seeing an Englishman behaving like a popinjay.

"He is obviously poor," snapped Delphine. "Clearly he has found he can make a living by his skills. Do not preach so, Maria. You make my head ache!"

Mrs. Bencastle was beginning to feel bewildered and anxious. Twice now the usually placid Lady Charteris had snapped at her.

As they reached the corner of Holles Street, the tiger appeared before them.

He thrust a pink rose at Delphine, said, "From the guvner," and scampered back into the crowd.

"Throw it away," said Mrs. Bencastle.

Delphine turned the long-stemmed rose around in her fingers and did not reply.

Mrs. Bencastle noticed that Delphine still carried the rose as she sat in the carriage on the road back to Bedfordshire. A crease of worry appeared between Maria Bencastle's thick eyebrows. First there had been Delphine's unexpected anger. And then this petty mountebank sending her a rose, a rose she still carried. It dawned on Mrs. Bencastle as she cast quick, sly glances at her companion that she had never realized before how pretty Delphine was! Her pretty sprigged muslin gown worn under a fitted pink sarcenet pelisse accentuated her excellent figure. Her pink straw bonnet with its crown of roses shaded a perfect oval of a face.

What if Delphine should marry again? And what if the new husband gave Mrs. Bencastle her marching orders?

For the first time in her life, Mrs. Bencastle realized she would have to set herself out to please. She had no desire to live on her own.

Marsham Manor was comfortable, almost luxurious, although Mrs. Bencastle would not admit, even to herself, that the added luxuries were a result of Delphine's excellent farm management.

The manor was a small, gracious Caroline mansion of mellow brick, standing in a mere twenty acres of formal garden. Beyond the gardens stretched the rich acres of farmland which Lady Charteris had learned to manage so well.

Although the house had been originally built in 1680, it had been redesigned and renovated in 1750 by Sir George Charteris's father. At that time, the country had once again become fashionable, and aristocrats no longer looked forward to a visit to their estates with all the enthusiasm they usually reserved for a visit to the dentist.

Farming, instead of being a chore to be turned over to stewards and tenant farmers, became the main interest of the landowner. Sir George had carried on that tradition and had found a willing pupil in Delphine.

He had been a gentle, courteous man whose bravery in rescuing so many French aristocrats from the guillotine had largely gone unsung. The child, Delphine de Fleuris, had been his last rescue mission.

From being a calm and courteous guardian, he had become a calm and courteous husband, and although the intimacies of marriage had aroused no great searing passions in Delphine, she had loved her husband dearly, had mourned him sincerely, and had never once thought of the possibility of marrying again.

She was relatively content with her isolated life. The local county might shun her, but she was adored by her tenant farmers and estate workers. Sometimes she found the work almost *too* hard, particularly when she was called in to settle petty disputes. Sir George had always been able to handle tricky matters like that with great ease. She spent long days in the saddle and long evenings poring over books on the latest farm machinery and methods of rearing livestock.

But on her return from the fair, after Mrs. Bencastle

and the servants had gone to bed, Delphine pushed open the french windows in the drawing room and went down the shallow, mossy steps into the garden.

It was a clear, cold night with stars burning in the heavens and a light breeze sending the first autumn leaves drifting onto the lawns.

A sundial glimmered whitely at the end of the walk, and the plop of a rising fish in the goldfish pond sounded startlingly loud in the night silence.

Delphine took a deep breath. The fair with its noise and color still seemed to dance before her eyes. With a little pang, she realized she had never been to a ball or a party. Sir George and Delphine had led a quiet, almost middle-aged sort of life. He had hired tutors for her. She had been taught to dance and to play the pianoforte and to paint tolerable watercolors. She had had an education Sir George considered suitable for a young lady. But she had had no stage in life on which to exhibit these talents.

Marsham Manor and the health of its lands and tenants had totally absorbed Sir George, and Delphine had made his interest her own.

It was a disloyal thought, but she could not help feeling for the first time that she had never been young.

The wind rustled through the ivy on the wall behind her, and she shivered in the cold air.

Tomorrow she would again be anesthetized by her daily labors: looking after cultivation and stock, attending market fairs, settling disputes, prescribing medicine from the stillroom for the infirm, and going into the neighboring town to attend a coal and clothing club where she kept the books and set down the savings of the poor.

She played a little with a dream where she would appoint a steward and go to London, attend all the plays and operas, and see the museums and the sights.

She had traveled to the fair in London without a

thought, without thinking that she was taking a monumental step.

Delphine shivered again and made her way indoors, snuffing out the candles in the drawing room and climbing the stairs to bed. The pink rose seemed to shine in a small vase beside her bed. She had despised that performer, but perhaps he knew better how to live than she did.

There was no real reason to martyr herself to the cares of the land for three hundred sixty-five days. Other estate owners took three months away from the country to "do" the Season, returning refreshed to the cares of crops and harvests.

But to take such a step, to make such a decision, would mean, Delphine thought wryly, that she was looking for a husband.

And why on earth would she want to sacrifice her freedom and property to some man?

But, almost unbidden, came a guilty memory of her behavior on the night before her wedding. She remembered crying in a desolate way for the loss of that romantic dream love; for the loss of that young, strong lover she had secretly hoped she might find some day.

That memory had been savagely thrust far down in her mind. She had told herself she was the luckiest girl in the world to be marrying her gentle and good Sir George. She had been happy and content with him. She sincerely missed him. But there had been something about the fair. Something about the frivolous gaiety of it all.

Delphine gave an extremely Gallic shrug. She must be tired. These were silly dreams, bad memories, and immature longings. Tomorrow the routine would begin again. Tomorrow she would forget her youth and her French heritage.

The days came and went, and the countryside sank into its long winter sleep. Mrs. Bencastle, reassured now that no suitor had appeared on the horizon, had reverted to her normal grumbling after a brief spell of trying to be pleasant, and Delphine had reverted to her former tolerant behavior and paid her no heed.

Gradually the fair faded to a pale memory, as faded and withered as the rose now pressed between the pages of *The Pig Breeders' Almanac*.

The winter was exceptionally severe, blinding blizzards followed by bone-hard frosts. Then, just when it seemed as if the whole of England had been moved to the North Pole, spring came sweeping across the countryside, sending the rivers tumbling and rushing through the brown earth of the fields. Day after sunny day brought out the new leaves, and the new corn covered the fields in a green mist.

The dripping hedgerows were alive with birdsong. Spring brought new life to the countryside and discontent into Delphine's heart.

The pleasant rooms of Marsham Manor were flooded with pale yellow sunlight. Fires still had to be lit, but the sunlight bleached the flames to pale ghosts of their winter's welcoming glare.

Delphine spent long days in the saddle but returned home in the evening still restless and—at last she had to admit it—bored to death.

Two of her tenant farmers, Mr. Yardley and Mr. Stone, paid her one of their frequent visits. They were always squabbling about boundary lines and refused to talk to each other, using Delphine as an interpreter. "Tell Yardley he's encroaching on my land," Farmer Stone would say, to which Farmer Yardley would reply, "My lady, tell Farmer Stone he is talking fustian."

Normally, Delphine found these strange interchanges exhausting and irritating, but that day, she found herself actually welcoming the diversion.

She was busily engaged in passing insults from one farmer to the other in the cluttered estates' office at the back of the house, when her butler, Bradley, came shuffling in. Like most of the servants, he was quite old and very set in his ways. Like all of the servants, he had transferred his crusty devotion for the late Sir George to his young widow.

"There are persons to see your ladyship," he said, addressing a bust of Plato on top of the bookcase. "*Foreign* persons, my lady."

"Her ladyship don't have no truck with furreners," said Farmer Yardley truculently.

"It's not Farmer Yardley's place to say who her ladyship should or should not see," responded Farmer Stone smugly.

"Who are these persons, Bradley?" asked Delphine. "Did they not present cards?"

"They did, my lady," said Bradley lugubriously, producing a small tray from behind his back on which reposed two visiting cards, each one with the corner neatly turned down to signify that the owner had called in person.

Delphine scanned the cards. One said "Le Marquis de Graux" and the other "M. Charles Renaud."

"Oh, but I must see them, Bradley," exclaimed Delphine, rising quickly. "Mr. Yardley and Mr. Stone will excuse me. Perhaps these are two of the gentlemen whose lives Sir George saved."

"Very well, my lady," Bradley said sourly as he left the office. He shared Mrs. Bencastle's views.

The two farmers rose quickly. They had no desire to be left alone together without their "interpreter."

When they had left, Delphine rang the bell. "Where have you put the gentlemen, Bradley?" she asked.

"In the hall, my lady."

"Show them into the drawing room immediately, Bradley," said Delphine severely. "You must not treat high-ranking French gentlemen like servants."

Bradley went out, muttering under his breath. Everyone around here seems to grumble the whole time, thought Delphine with sudden impatience.

Sometimes in the past when Delphine was still a child, a few French aristocrats had called to see Sir George. He had never allowed her to be present. Sir George had said it was better that Delphine should be reared entirely as an English miss. He had allowed her to be taught French, since that was part of any young lady's education. But he really feared that the sight of her compatriots would remind Delphine of the terrors she had endured. Sir George had never talked to her of her parents' death or of how he had come to rescue her.

When she was older, she had tried to tell him that *not* knowing was worse than any horror he could tell her, but he had only shaken his head and said in his gentle voice that he would tell her one day. But he had died, and she still did not know.

She herself could remember nothing. Her earliest memories were of Marsham Manor.

She walked into the drawing room and looked at the two gentlemen who had risen to meet her. They were very old. Their dress was shabby and antiquated. Both wore old blue coats, marseillaise waistcoats and knee breeches with clumsy buckled shoes.

They introduced themselves in strongly accented English. The Marquis de Graux was small and spry with a cloud of snow white hair tied at the nape of his neck with a black ribbon. Monsieur Renaud was small and fat and wheezed as he bowed. His eyes were pale blue and innocent like the eyes of a child.

"Delphine de Fleuris," said the marquis. "I can hardly believe my eyes. You are the image of your mother."

"You knew my mother?" asked Delphine, sitting down and motioning them to do the same.

"Yes, we were close friends of your family in the old days before the Terror," said the marquis. "We thought you had died with your parents or we would have come to you sooner. Then someone saw you at

14

a fair in Cavendish Square last September. It was held to benefit our people. This lady, a Madame Beauchair, who had known your mother, swore that she had seen you, that you must be alive.

"It took us many long months to trace you. *Hélas!* It appears we are too late. You are the Lady Charteris. You are married!"

"My husband is dead," said Delphine, noticing with surprise the sudden relief on the two old faces opposite. "How did my parents die?" she asked quickly. "Sir George would never tell me."

The marquis looked at her for a long moment, his small black eyes shrewd and assessing. "It is not a pretty story, milady. In brief, you know you are from Fleuris, in the Loire region?"

Delphine nodded. "That much I do know, Monsieur le Marquis, but nothing else."

"*Eh bien.* Your parents tried to escape from the château before the mob reached them, but they were too late. They were driven back with pitchforks into the château. Your father was holding you in his arms. The doors of the château were barricaded, and the mob surrounded the building.

"They set it on fire.

"At one point, your mother appeared at the window. She begged the crowd to spare your life. They jeered at her.

"At another, a man was seen running over the roof. The crowd threw stones at him. He tied a rope to one of the gargoyles and swung over and crashed through an upstairs window.

"He was dismissed as a madman, some crazy servant who wished to die with his masters. We now believe it was Sir George Charteris."

Delphine put her hands over her eyes. For one brief moment, she thought she felt the scorching heat and heard the dreadful, dreadful screaming that never seemed to stop.

"I am sorry," said the marquis wearily. He seemed to have seen and lived through many horrors. "Perhaps I should have spared you. We of the French *émigrés* are become morbid. Often we talk of such terrible things over and over again until they have no real meaning for us anymore."

"*Nous sommes vieux*," said Monsieur Renaud with a deprecating smile.

"Yes, we are old," agreed the marquis sadly. "But we did not come to tell you of such *tristes* affairs." He produced a bundle of papers yellow with age.

"We are come to carry out your dear parents' last wishes."

"You have a letter? Something they wrote to me before they died?" said Delphine eagerly.

"No. Legal documents. Your parents' lawyer escaped their fate and brought all his papers with him. He died in London and left them in the care of Madame Beauchair."

"And what is the content of these papers, Monsieur le Marquis?"

The marquis crackled open the parchment.

"In short..." he began.

The door of the drawing room opened, and Mrs. Bencastle marched in. As usual she was dressed from head to foot in black.

The Frenchmen rose at her entrance and were introduced by Delphine.

Mrs. Bencastle sniffed and sat down next to Delphine on a straw-colored sofa and glared at the visitors.

"These gentlemen have legal documents from my parents," said Delphine. "Monsieur le Marquis was just about to tell me their import when you arrived."

"How do you know they're genuine?" muttered Mrs. Bencastle.

"Oh, *Maria!*" exclaimed Delphine impatiently.

"I should explain first, milady," said the marquis,

"that it was quite usual for couples to be betrothed in France—and still is—when they were very young."

Delphine and Mrs. Bencastle sat very still, staring at him.

"*En effet*, what I am trying to say is that your parents betrothed you to the Comte Saint-Pierre exactly one year before they died. The Comte Saint-Pierre was some ten years older than you, milady, at the time. His father's estates marched on those of your father. It was to be a *mariage de convenance, vous voyez*."

"Speak English," barked Mrs. Bencastle.

Delphine put out a restraining hand. "The Marquis de Graux is saying that it was to be a marriage of convenience, Maria. Go on, Monsieur le Marquis. We have such marriages in England as well. But usually when the couple is older, of course. And this poor Comte Saint-Pierre. I assume he died in the Terror as well?"

"On the contrary, milady," said Monsieur Renaud. "He is living in London. He has learned of your existence, and he is waiting to marry you."

Chapter Two

❖

There was complete and absolute silence.

Then a log shifted in the grate, and an old clock gave a gentle whirring sound preparatory to striking the hour.

Mrs. Bencastle was the first to find her voice.

"Stuff," she said roundly. "Lady Charteris is English and was married to my sainted brother, God rest his soul. I suppose this Comte Saint-Peer has no money?"

"No," said Monsieur Renaud innocently. "Like very many of us, he has practically nothing."

"Well, there you are!" burst out Mrs. Bencastle. "A trick if ever I heard one. Plaguey bunch of mountebanks barging into decent English homes and . . ."

"Maria! Leave us," said Delphine quietly.

"That I shall not. Leave an innocent lamb like you to . . ."

"To see that my guests are treated with the courtesy they deserve," said Delphine firmly. "I am perfectly

18

well able to handle my own affairs, Maria. Go. And do not breathe a word of this to *anyone*."

"As if I would..."

"As you might in the way that you have gossiped before about my Frenchness and my unmaidenly behavior in running the estates myself. People talk behind *your* back as well, Maria. I am kept quite *au fait* with all your criticisms."

Mrs. Beñcastle opened her mouth, shut it again, and stumped from the room.

"Now..." Delphine turned to her visitors. "Please let me see the documents."

They were silently handed over, and Delphine studied them carefully. At last, she put them down with a sigh.

"Yes, they are authentic," she said. "I *sense* they are. But what can I do? I run these estates very profitably. If I marry, all will go to my husband. What if he should be a wastrel? I have not only my own life to consider but the lives of my servants and tenants. What does the Comte Saint-Pierre do for his livelihood?"

A slightly embarrassed glance was exchanged between the two old gentlemen, and then Monsieur Renaud said gently, "He teaches fencing and... and ... quite a number of other things.

"He is of sterling character. Had he turned bad, we would not have approached you. We do not ask for money for ourselves. But think, milady, we feel honor bound to tell you of your parents' wishes. Perhaps, of course, France is no longer your country. Perhaps you feel no loyalty to the pitiful remnants of the French aristocracy. But to us, these family arrangements are as binding as they were to your parents. Had they been alive, then you and the Comte Saint-Pierre would most certainly have been married."

Delphine rose and walked over to the window and stood for a moment, looking out. So many things to assimilate at once. Her parents' death—burned alive, dear God. And now marriage! It was unthinkable. Marsham Manor was all about her, its quiet, elegant rooms with the portraits of the Charteris family looking down at her solemnly with their painted eyes. The garden beyond, gilded with sunlight. How could she be so ungrateful?

Ungrateful, because all this comfort and order felt like a cage. Oh, that these gentlemen had never called. Oh, that she had never gone to that fair.

It was madness to even consider marriage to a man she had never met. And yet her parents had wished it. A vision of her mother holding her at the window of the château and pleading for her life, while the mob roared and the hungry flames licked at the building, assailed her. And this comte. Impoverished and far from his native land...

She came to a decision.

"Gentlemen," she said, "I cannot possibly give you any reply at the moment. Please stay here as my guests for a few days. It will give me time to give you my answer."

"You are very kind, my lady," said Monsieur Renaud. "It would be pleasant to rest in the English countryside."

Delphine rang the bell for Bradley and informed the butler to arrange rooms for the two guests. After they had gone, she sat down at a writing desk by one of the windows and studied the legal documents carefully.

As in English legal documents, there were a great deal of heretofores and wherefores, but the message was plain. Delphine was surprised to find herself reading the French with ease. She herself, as she knew, was the only daughter of the Baron de Fleuris and his wife, Félice.

Jules Saint-Pierre was the only son of the late Comte Saint-Pierre. He had taken the title on his father's death. Delphine's parents had paid a great deal of money by way of marriage settlements to the comte. How strange to think that had the Revolution not happened she would be a young French lady, attending the court at Versailles with her husband.

But it was all so long ago. Surely she was as English as ... as Mrs. Bencastle.

But when Mrs. Bencastle strode into the room and demanded harshly to know whether Delphine had put an end to this French nonsense, adding that it was madness to even consider marriage to some penniless "Frenchie," Delphine felt her temper rising. Once more Maria Bencastle was beginning to irritate her as she had never done before. All at once, Delphine felt like a schoolroom miss being perpetually berated by a grumpy governess who had been allowed too much license.

"Maria," said Delphine, putting down the documents, "you forget that I *am* French, and 'fore George, I'm proud of it!

"I have no intention of dismissing my dead parents' wishes out of hand. Try for a little sympathy. It is the first time I have ever learned the nature of their deaths. And although it all happened so long ago, the shock is still very great. You are not to interfere or try in any way to influence my decision, Maria. No! Not another word. These gentlemen, who are our guests, are to be treated with kindness and courtesy. I have told them I will give them my answer in several days."

"Have you forgotten George so soon?" demanded Mrs. Bencastle.

A tender smile curled Delphine's lips. "I could never forget George. Never! I will always love him, Maria, and cherish his memory. Come. Let us not be at odds. I will put aside the matter until this evening. I must ride over to see Mrs. Jones and take her some rose water and some medicine." Mrs. Jones was one of the farm laborers' wives.

Delphine was glad to escape from the house and from Mrs. Bencastle's disapproving presence.

She was dressed in a garment known as a "joseph." The joseph was cut like a coachman's greatcoat, but the capes were on a lesser scale. On her head, she wore a drab beaver bonnet. It was her working dress. Her slight figure atop her great mare, Xerxes, was a familiar sight around the countryside.

Although her lands had prospered under her good stewardship, a great deal of money had come from sales of wheat in 1812, when it sold at the famine price of one hundred twenty-six shillings and sixpence a quarter. Delphine had used the money from the sales to make sure that every man, woman, and child on her estates had had enough to eat. Although she had done this from the best motives, it had saved her from the laborers' riots which had ruined many a more clutch-fisted landowner's property. On many another estate, when there was a bad harvest, the workers starved. And the harvests had been dreadful.

In only six of the twenty-one years between 1793 and the previous year, 1814, was an average harvest gathered.

Though more land was laid down to corn than ever before, the supply was not large enough to feed the people of England, and death from starvation was not uncommon. Although the war had ended and Napoleon was in exile on the island of Elba, conditions had not improved.

Sir George had adopted the pioneering methods of Coke of Norfolk and had improved the farming, despite the bad harvests. He marled and clayed the land, using a great deal of purchased manure, adopted the four-course rotation, grew wheat where only rye had grown before, grew turnips, clover, and sainfoin. By these means, he was also able to increase his number of livestock.

Delphine paid her call on Mrs. Jones and then rode

on into the local market town of Littlejohn. The air was clear and warm, and the hard riding had enabled her to put the problems brought about by the French gentlemen's visit aside for the moment.

But there seemed to be a great excitement in the normally sleepy town. People stood in knots at corners, talking earnestly. Others were studying a bulletin posted up outside the offices of the *Littlejohn Recorder*.

Delphine dismounted outside the inn, the Wheatsheaf, in the town square.

Mr. Partington, who owned the haberdashery, came bustling up. "Terrible news, my lady," he said. "Terrible."

"What is it?" asked Delphine with some amusement, since Mr. Partington always met her with this greeting. It usually turned out to be a piece of town gossip of minor importance.

"Boney's escaped!" gasped Mr. Partington. "'Tis said he has landed in the south of France and none can stop his march."

"Wellington will stop him," said Delphine, although she felt a shiver of fear. Napoleon Bonaparte had been an ogre who had haunted her childhood.

She could still remember the panic when it was thought that Napoleon would invade England. But they had lived with the war for so long, and last year it seemed as if Napoleon would never rise again.

Mr. Partington went on his way to spread the news to a more rewarding audience, and Delphine stood lost in thought.

The threat of being at war again, although she was in no way involved, brought an increase in the restless excitement that had begun to plague her. War brought with it thoughts of death, thoughts of the mortality of man; brought with it a realization that the days were slipping and sliding and gliding towards old age without excitement, without *fun*. Never had Delphine felt so young.

She became aware that someone was watching her and looked around.

Mr. Garnett, steward to the Bryce-Connells, Marsham Manor's most prosperous neighbors, was standing revolving his hat between his fingers and studying her anxiously.

"Good day, Mr. Garnett." Delphine smiled on him. She did not approve of his master, Mr. Bryce-Connell, who had a reputation of being harsh to his tenants and servants. Mr. Garnett, however, was known to be a good steward. It was said that the Bryce-Connell estates would never have survived the bad harvests under less expert management than that of Mr. Garnett.

"I would beg the favor of a word with you, my lady," said Mr. Garnett. "Perhaps I might have your permission to call. It's on a matter of business."

"Very well," said Delphine with a little sigh, thinking it was probably some lengthy matter of cattle straying onto Mr. Bryce-Connell's land. "Perhaps we could discuss it now?"

"Yes, my lady," mumbled Mr. Garnett in a manner very far removed from his usual cheerfulness.

"Then let us go into the Wheatsheaf," said Delphine, leading the way.

Mr. Garnett followed her. It was strange, he thought, that such a young lady as Lady Charteris should perpetually ride about without a maid.

Delphine began to sense that Mr. Garnett's business matter might be something out of the common way and so she asked for a private parlor.

When they were both seated over a bottle of wine and a tray of biscuits, she settled herself down to listen to Mr. Garnett, who seemed strangely reluctant to begin.

At last she prompted gently, "Perhaps Mr. Bryce-Connell has some complaint . . . ?"

"Oh, my lady," burst out Mr. Garnett. "He has, indeed, and the complaint is about me. I have lost my employ."

Delphine looked in surprise at his honest, square face. "You know Mr. Bryce-Connell often loses his temper and says things in haste which he repents at leisure," she said. It was unthinkable, after all, that Bryce-Connell should rid himself of such a valuable steward.

"We've been quarreling for some time, my lady," said Mr. Garnett in a low voice. "Mr. Bryce-Connell and I never saw eye to eye over the tenants' welfare. Somehow I managed to look after them. Now he says if there is no work for the laborers, then they are not to be paid.

"I know it's the law, my lady, and that he's within his rights. But it's mortal hard to see people suffering for want of food. Well, we had words, and his sister Miss Harriet ups and says that Mr. Bryce-Connell is a milksop to allow a servant to speak to him in that way—meaning me, my lady. And so I lost my employ."

"And you are come to me for work?" asked Delphine.

"Oh, and it please your ladyship, *any* kind of work."

"You are an educated man, Mr. Garnett," said Delphine thoughtfully, "and you have a good reputation. It should be easy for you to find another position."

"Mr. Bryce-Connell will not give me a reference. He says I am a thief. And it's a lie, my lady," said Mr. Garnett passionately. "They—that's Mr. Bryce-Connell and his sister—say a gold statuette was found in my room. I swore blind I never touched it, but they said I should consider myself lucky that they had not taken me to the nearest roundhouse."

A light breeze blew in at the open window, bringing with it all the scents of early spring.

"I shall employ you," said Delphine suddenly and abruptly, her voice almost harsh.

"My lady!" gasped Mr. Garnett. "I would be honored to work for you."

"You will work as my steward, Mr. Garnett, and you may hire an assistant as well. For your assistant, I would like you to look among the young men on my estate and find one that you think worthy of education and advancement. I shall supply you with some names, of course, but I would like the decision to be yours.

"This comes at a very opportune moment. I trust you will not repeat this conversation to anyone, but I have become wearied of the chores of my own stewardship. The country people have accepted me, but they would rather be governed by a man. I—I have in mind a certain undertaking, which means I shall perhaps be not as well able to attend to things as I was in the past. You may commence your duties immediately. I gather you are at liberty to do so?"

"Yes, my lady. I was turned out of my dwelling this morning."

"How very like Mr. Bryce-Connell," said Delphine. "He is like one of those wicked squires so beloved of Astley's Amphitheatre that I read about in the newspapers—constantly turning people out into the snow.

"It is hard to believe such people exist in real life, but I am still inclined to expect everyone to be like my late husband."

"I would to God they were," said Mr. Garnett fervently. "He was the finest man the county has ever known."

"Then I shall expect you in my estates' office later today, Mr. Garnett. I will explain as much as I can and will take you on a tour of the estates tomorrow."

After she had parted from Mr. Garnett, she attended the coal and clothing club, and then made her way back to the main square.

She was about to mount her horse when she saw Mr. Bryce-Connell and his sister, Harriet, alighting from their carriage. They saw her at the same time.

26

Harriet's beautiful lips curled in a complacent smile as her blue gaze took in the drabness of Lady Charteris's clothes. She herself was wearing a Bourbon hat and mantle—named to celebrate the return of the royal family to Paris. Her hat was made of blue satin trimmed with fleur-de-lis in pearls; an edging of floss silk and pearls finished the brim and a white ostrich feather was placed on one side. Fleur-de-lis trimmed both the Bourbon dress and mantle.

Harriet's blond curls peeped out from under her delicious bonnet. Her fair English complexion glowed with health. Delphine was conscious all of a sudden of the dowdiness of her own dress and the foreignness of her coloring.

Mr. Bryce-Connell was stocky and florid. He was as fair as his sister, but his blue eyes were crisscrossed with red veins, and his high color owed more to port than health.

He assumed a mincing, affected manner which did not go well with his burly farmer's figure.

"Servant, Lady Charteris," he simpered. "'Pon rep, it is a good thing we have Wellington to fight for us. Those demned Frenchies are like black beetles. Can't get rid of 'em. Stamp 'em down one place and they pop up another."

"La!" Harriet smiled. "You forget, Lady Charteris is French."

"Oh, she'll have forgotten all of that nonsense." Mr. Bryce-Connell giggled.

"Much as I would adore to stand here and listen to you both maligning my race and character," said Delphine, swinging herself up into the side saddle, "I fear I must bid you adieu. It is amazing, is it not, that the English who most affect to despise the French wear French fashions and interlard their conversation with bad French? But I have business to attend to. You see, Mr. Garnett will be working for me."

"Garnett! The man's a thief," cried Mr. Bryce-Connell.

"Oh, the gold statuette. He told me about that. Of course, I did not believe a word of it. One would have to be quite mad to think Mr. Garnett would steal anything."

And with a small bow from the waist, Delphine spurred her horse and rode off quickly before either of the Bryce-Connells could find time to reply.

"Monstrous!" said Harriet angrily, staring after the slight figure on horseback, now at the far end of the square.

"She called us *liars*! And the statuette was found in Garnett's bedchamber."

"Where you put it," said her brother. "An unnecessary touch, that."

"Pah!" said Harriet disdainfully. "Unnecessary, indeed. You needed something to have against him. If I had not interceded, he would have had the whole estate overrun with paupers, eating us out of house and home. You should have had Garnett charged with the theft. Now the wretched man will make the Charteris estates prosper just to get his revenge."

"We'll find a way to make Lady Charteris smart," said her brother thoughtfully. "I don't know why people hereabouts won't hear a word against her. She's French. She behaves like a farmer. And she has not one ounce of femininity in her whole body!"

But Delphine was feeling the disadvantages of her sex very much indeed. If she were a man, she thought savagely, she would have challenged Mr. Bryce-Connell to a duel on the spot. Somehow, however, they had contrived to make her feel like a foreigner in a strange country. For the first time, she began to think of herself as French.

All at once, the facts of her parents' death hit her like a hammer blow. She reined in Xerxes and slowly bent her head forward until her face was buried in the animal's shaggy mane and cried her eyes out.

She had a sudden longing to have a companion, some man who would take some of the cares of her life from her shoulders. Someone to turn to and lean on. Someone French who would understand that one could not shed one's nationality even after a long stay in England.

Would a marriage of convenience be such a bad thing? Delphine dried her eyes and slowly looked about at the budding trees and hedgerows. The sun was going down in flaming glory behind a bank of clouds. Red light washed over the fields, making the landscape look strange and alien. What was this Comte Saint-Pierre like? He was not a wastrel. Somehow she trusted the two elderly Frenchmen's judgment on that score. She felt she could almost see him. Someone dark-haired and golden-skinned like her, with quick, vital gestures talking rapid French.

She rode on until she came to the top of Hebcock Hill, one of the few hills in the flat countryside.

Marsham Manor lay below her surrounded by trees, lit by the setting sun. Smoke curled up lazily from its tall chimneys.

From a nearby cottage came the sound of children's laughter. Children! It had seemed odd that she and Sir George had not been blessed with children. At first she had cried, feeling she was less than a woman, that it was all somehow her own fault, and Sir George had laughed and pulled her down onto his lap and ruffled her curls, saying she was the only child he needed in his life.

But she was not a child, thought Delphine sadly, but a woman with all of a woman's longings and passions. And although there could be no great, passionate love to be expected from an arranged marriage, perhaps it would bring children and companionship.

All at once she was eager to get home and see more

of her guests and hear more about her parents. She urged Xerxes into a gallop.

Maria Bencastle was sourer than she had ever been before. Nothing but French was spoken at the dinner table. This steward had been appointed without consulting *her*, and not only that, he had hired an assistant—a mere cottage youth with only a smattering of education.

She had told Mr. Garnett firmly that all problems should be brought to her. Lady Charteris took too much upon herself. But Mr. Garnett had simply smiled and continued to go to Delphine for advice.

Certainly the conversation at the dining table had begun in English, the others being too polite to wish to exclude her from the conversation. But she had tried to put these unwanted guests in their place by saying, "Since you speak English so badly, why don't you speak in French? It will not trouble me at all, I can assure you." They had been about to protest, but Delphine had flashed her an enigmatic look and had begun to talk in French and, it seemed, had not stopped since.

Mrs. Bencastle's only allies were the servants, but they were too much in awe of their young mistress to do anything to make these wretched Frenchmen feel unwelcome. Mrs. Bencastle's only consolation was that as far as she could gather, no further mention had been made of this stupid marriage arrangement.

But the subject had been much discussed—in French. The Marquis de Graux told Delphine how the young Jules Saint-Pierre had been forced to watch his parents being guillotined. He had been destined to follow them on the following day, but a soft-hearted turnkey at the Bastille had smuggled him out in a suit of rags, pretending that he was a peasant boy who had been found skulking about.

He told her how the young comte had made his way bit by bit towards England, working on farms to gather a little money, then working his passage to England. He was a gallant young man, said the marquis, and as brave as a lion.

He also told her at length about her parents, talking of the château in the Loire Valley, talking of happier times, describing them in detail to Delphine, never again touching on the agony of their death.

That night, when Delphine fell asleep, she had a vivid dream of her mother, pretty and powdered, holding out rounded arms and teasing her to take her first steps. She could even feel the sun warm on her back and see the exquisite embroidery of her mother's panniered gown and the way the sun shone on her powdered hair.

She awoke with a start and lay trembling. It had all seemed so real. She lay in the darkness and thought about all the conversation of the evening. Thought about how French came so naturally to her lips, and about how the presence of the two elderly Frenchmen had managed to banish her feeling of foreignness and isolation.

And then she thought about this Comte Saint-Pierre. It would be a marriage in name only, insisted the Marquis de Graux. He was only interested in carrying out her dead parents' wishes.

The pull of the past was very strong. Perhaps if Sir George had made an effort to introduce his young bride to the homes of the county or had taken her to London for a season, Delphine would not have felt so isolated after his death. But after he had rescued her, Sir George had become something of a recluse as far as the social world was concerned, and so, in a way, he became England for Delphine; and on his death, she once again felt foreign, one of the despised French unable to take root on English soil.

Now she began to realize why the French *émigrés* flocked together, only speaking French, hanging on to the hope that one day their estates would be restored, that one day they would return to the sunshine of France and leave England with its fog and perpetual roast beef behind.

All at once, Delphine made up her mind to go ahead with the marriage.

She must trust her parents' judgment, and the high opinion of the Comte Saint-Pierre which her two guests evidently had.

After being hard-working and quiet and practical all her life, Delphine felt a tingle of excitement at the idea of taking such a plunge into unknown waters.

Monsieur Renaud had said that if she decided to marry the Comte Saint-Pierre, then they would return immediately to London to tell him the news. Since it was not necessary that she meet the comte first, as it was to be a marriage of convenience, she could leave all arrangements for a quiet, modest wedding to the two gentlemen.

Delphine decided she would not mention anything about it to Maria Bencastle. Maria would only know about it when she returned home with her new husband.

It was this desire not to tell Maria Bencastle that made Delphine forego a meeting with her husband before the wedding. Underneath this reason was the wish not to have her glorious dream of a handsome, vital, dashing French nobleman destroyed. Deep down, Delphine craved romance and frivolity.

Mrs. Bencastle smiled for the first time, showing strong yellow teeth as Delphine's traveling carriage eventually departed, bearing the two French gentlemen off to London.

They had come by the stage, and Mrs. Bencastle had seen no reason why they should not leave that way, but Delphine had insisted that they take the carriage.

"Oooof!" huffed Maria Bencastle. "Good riddance. Now I can be comfortable again." And so by way of making herself comfortable, she went in search of Delphine to complain about the two old gentlemen and to treat that young lady to a harangue on the unscrupulous, un-English behavior of the French. Delphine listened to all this with her former stoic calm, and Mrs. Bencastle felt more than ever that life had returned to normal.

A week passed, and Mrs. Bencastle found she could not keep such a delicious piece of gossip to herself. Harriet Bryce-Connell would gladly serve a delicious tea in return for such a fascinating piece of news.

She dressed accordingly in her best black silk, seized her beloved umbrella, and informed Delphine that she wished the use of the landau to "make a few calls."

Delphine graciously inclined her head, suppressing a sigh of relief. For she had planned to leave for London that day and had already been thinking up various ruses to keep Maria away until she had effected her departure. Now no lies would be necessary.

But Delphine could not resist calling sweetly after Mrs. Bencastle as she heaved her bulk into the landau, "Do not forget to tell *dear* Harriet all about my French visitors."

"As if I would," said Mrs. Bencastle, turning puce.

"As if you wouldn't," murmured Delphine as the landau bore Mrs. Bencastle away.

Now to London... and her wedding day.

Delphine had made her plans carefully. Her servants were to leave her at Madame Beauchair's flat in Manchester Square and then return immediately with the carriage to Marsham Manor.

They were to tell Mrs. Bencastle that she had decided to stay in London for a few days. Madame Beauchair had made all the arrangements. Her modest flat was to serve for Delphine's wedding night.

Delphine did not for a moment imagine any intimacy taking place between herself and her husband until perhaps they came to know each other very well. But she was reluctant to return with him immediately after the wedding to Marsham Manor.

Reality began to gnaw at the edges of Delphine's dream as soon as the carriage rolled away and she was left alone with Madame Beauchair.

Madame Beauchair was a middle-aged lady of quite terrifying gentility. She spoke French in a low whisper, as if frightened of being overheard, until Delphine ended up practically shouting at her in the hope that her own raised voice would heighten the ghostly whisper of Madame Beauchair's.

Madame Beauchair was timid and faded. Her clothes were very elaborate and very grand and very worn. The lace at her neck and wrists was yellow with age, and her silk gown had once been cut to accommodate the large hooped panniers of the last century, and, without its hoops, it trailed along the ground at her feet in great folds of dusty material.

Then the flat was rather like its occupant. It was sparsely furnished, with everything seeming dull and threadbare. There was one small servant who acted as housemaid, cook, parlor maid, and lady's maid, a thin red-handed waif of a creature who started at shadows. Madame Beauchair ordered the girl here and there as if commanding a whole army of servants.

But she stressed the joy of carrying out poor Félice's wishes so much—Félice being Delphine's late mother—that Delphine found she had not the courage to protest that the whole idea had been a terrible mistake.

And yet, as they were ready to leave for the church, she was seized with a desire to escape. It was as if the fresh air and sunshine outside had restored her to normality. The whole thing was preposterous! She must have been mad. She was on her way to marry some man she had never set eyes on. *Preposterous*!

She took a deep breath of spring air and turned to tell Madame Beauchair so, but she found that lady looking at her with tears in her eyes and whispering,

"I am so happy. Dear Félice. Her sacrifice was not in vain."

"Sacrifice?" Delphine looked at Madame Beauchair with wide, haunted eyes.

"Oh, yes. Dear Monsieur le Marquis said it was believed she could have escaped, but she and your father stood at the window, looking down at the mob, until the flames engulfed them. Monsieur le Marquis believes now that they did that so that Sir George could manage to carry you to safety while the crowd's attention was fixed on themselves. But they did not die in vain! Delphine de Fleuris is to marry the Comte Saint-Pierre at last."

Numbly, Delphine bowed her head, an odd little bow of assent. She could never voice her doubts now.

As the hired hack bore them towards the church, Delphine wondered if her gown was not too severe. She was wearing a gray silk, high-waisted gown with triple flounces at the hem and a gauzy pereline of sky blue muslin about her shoulders. Her bonnet was a tiny confection of ribbons and artificial flowers, and her glossy brown curls had been dressed in a simple style.

Perhaps her husband would expect her to appear in a bride's gown.

The church was in a quiet alley near Soho Square, a small soot-blackened church which looked as if it were slowly sinking into the ground.

The Marquis de Graux was to give her away, with Madame Beauchair acting as maid of honor. Monsieur Renaud was to perform the duties of bride's man.

Delphine's arm trembled in that of the Marquis de Graux as he led her into the gloom of the small, empty church.

Two figures stood before the priest at the altar. Monsieur Renaud and her future husband.

Delphine received only a vague impression that he was very tall and very fair.

There were no organ, no flowers, and no choir.

In a dream, she mechanically made her responses, not once looking up at the tall figure next to her. At one moment during the service, a fit of hysteria seized her mind.

Naturally they had not thought she would need any rehearsal. After all, she had been married before!

She emerged as if from a dream when she held out her hand for the ring as she heard herself pronounced the wife of the Comte Saint-Pierre.

Delphine looked full into the face of her new husband for the first time.

And drew in her breath on a sharp gasp of disbelief.

She had seen those lazy blue eyes before, had seen that handsome aquiline face.

The last time she had seen him, he had been juggling silver balls in the middle of Cavendish Square.

It was the performer!

Here was no dark and virile Frenchman, but a tall man who looked as English as the countryside around Marsham Manor. An English-looking gentleman who was a juggler—and a clown.

Chapter Three

❖

———

Delphine's first frantic thought was how to make the best of this bad bargain. She no longer felt French. She felt like an outraged English matron. Why on earth had she not insisted on meeting the man first! But she had wanted her dream, and the two old gentlemen had also seemed very anxious to keep the couple apart until the day of the wedding. Looking back, Delphine felt she had been subjected to a bout of madness. For the first time in her life, she would have welcomed the blunt speech and squat, reassuring figure of Maria Bencastle.

They tricked me! was her predominant thought. No gentleman, French or English, who was worth his salt would perform before the common crowd.

The wedding party walked a short way to a coffee house where a private room had been hired for the wedding breakfast.

Delphine sat silently, hardly tasting her food, never

37

looking at her husband, while her French guests ate and ate.

At first they tried to draw her into the conversation, but after a while they gave up and talked among themselves of friends and acquaintances that Delphine did not know.

Her husband spoke in French, his light, amused voice rattling away. It seemed odd that such an English-looking man should be French.

At times, towards the end of the meal, he turned to her and spoke to her in English, pressing her to take more food and wine, which Delphine rudely and mulishly refused.

At last it was time for them to leave. Madame Beauchair was accompanying the two French gentlemen. Delphine and her new husband were to return to Manchester Square.

As they stood outside the coffee house, the Marquis de Graux drew Delphine a little aside. "You appear upset, Madame la Comtesse," he said.

"This man," said Delphine in a fierce whisper, "I have seen before. He was performing like any common mountebank at a fair. I believed you when you told me he was of sterling character."

"*Ma foi!* You are hard," cried the Marquis de Graux. "We must eat and make what money we can. We cannot eat dignity!"

"But there are other ways to make money," said Delphine savagely. "I have been tricked."

"No," said the Marquis de Graux sadly. "I swear you have not..."

He broke off as the Comte Saint-Pierre joined them, having commandeered a hack.

Delphine climbed in, shrugging off her husband's hand as he would have assisted her. He took his place beside her, hauling down the glass and shouting cheerfully to the Marquis de Graux, Monsieur Renaud, and Madame Beauchair. Then he sank back in the carriage seat and turned a bewitching smile on Delphine's stormy face.

"We will talk soon," he said gently. "Not now."

Delphine maintained a grim silence until they were back in the shabby flat in Manchester Square.

She became burningly conscious of the double bed in the next room. Matters must be sorted out as soon as possible.

She sat down and surveyed her new husband.

Jules Saint-Pierre was, just as she had remembered him, very tall and very rakish. His eyes were blue and fringed with long, curling lashes. He had a proud nose, a mobile mouth, which curled easily into a mocking smile, and thick, guinea-gold fair hair confined at the nape of the neck with a black ribbon.

He was wearing a blue morning coat with a striped waistcoat, canary yellow breeches, and Hessian boots. The clothes were new.

He leaned back in an armchair, rested his head on the back, and looked under sleepy lids at his fulminating bride.

"Out with it, *ma cherie*," he said. "I confess I should like to go to bed and sleep and sleep and sleep. But I cannot rest with such a prickly rose as yourself obviously waiting to tell me what a dreadful mistake you have made. Now, what is there about me that is so shocking, I wonder? I am not a hunchback, I am not a drunkard, I have no money—but that you knew already.... Come, choke it out."

Delphine removed her bonnet and set it very carefully on a table next to her.

"You, sir, are a mountebank!" she said. Maria Bencastle would have been proud of her.

"Go on."

"I have seen you before..."

"Could I ever forget," he interrupted.

"...at a street fair *juggling balls*."

"Like this?" He dug into the pocket in the tails of

39

his coat and produced six colored balls, which he proceeded to juggle in the air.

"Stop!" cried Delphine.

"Very well," he said, recapturing the balls and putting them back in his pocket. "I must make a living, you know. We have all not been as fortunate as Delphine de Fleuris."

"Could you please try for a little dignity," demanded Delphine, her color rising.

"I can't afford it, my sweeting. I am a good conjurer, and a good juggler. In between giving fencing lessons, French classes, and boxing lessons, I perform at street fairs. I am very successful. But the winters are hard."

"And how do you plan to gain money now?"

He leaned his head back on the chair again and crossed his long fingers over his waistcoat.

"By being married to you," he said simply.

"Does it not affect your pride that a woman should keep you?"

He stifled a yawn. "Not in the slightest. I have worked and worked and worked ever since I escaped Madame Guillotine. Tell me, Delphine, do you never long to play?"

"No," lied Delphine, stubbornly forcing down all her recent longings for amusement and frivolity. "I work very hard managing the estates at Marsham Manor."

"Do you not entertain?"

"I have no time for such things!"

"Oh, my dear," he said, sighing, "state your terms and let's have an end to it. I confess when Madame Beauchair told me afterwards that the dazzling brunette who had given me a whole guinea at the fair was none other than Delphine de Fleuris, I thought the sun was shining on my foggy English world for the first time. But, mark you, I am not of a mind to be nagged come sunup and sundown. The marriage can be annulled. Why should we be martyrs to our dead parents' wishes?"

Delphine suddenly felt ashamed of herself. But the shadow of the large bed in the next room loomed large in her mind and she said hurriedly, "Well...well, we shall see how we rub along. But I must make one thing clear. This is to be a marriage of convenience in *every* respect. I shall provide you with a home and the...the elegances of life, and you, in return, must engage to keep to your part of the bargain. I loved Sir George Charteris, my late husband, dearly, and can never love anyone again. Nor do I wish to try."

"Tut-tut!" he said lazily. "There is but one bed, Delphine, in the middle of a wilderness of curst uncomfortable furniture, but since I agree to your terms, I see no reason why we cannot share it. You are not going to be precisely driven mad with wild passion, are you? No. And only consider, my love, how little the ladies wear in the streets and how very much they wear in bed."

"My dear sir, this is no joking matter!"

"I was not joking," he said plaintively.

"And I accept your terms," he continued. "Just so long as you don't keep yammering at me and pouting in that way that quite ruins the shape of your delicious mouth. The shadow of the bulldog lies heavy upon you. When I look at you, I seem to see that stern guardian-lady who scowled so much over your shoulder at the fair."

"You will meet her when we return to Marsham," said Delphine. "She is Mrs. Bencastle, Sir George's sister."

"Ah, yes. Every pretty maiden should have a dragon."

"You will not find me ungenerous," said Delphine, determined to be fair. "We will call on my lawyers tomorrow. I informed them of my forthcoming marriage by letter."

"My sweet, were I the mountebank and wastrel you think me," he said gently, "I could take every penny from you. By this act of marriage, all you have becomes mine."

"I will kill you," said Delphine, her eyes flashing, "if you ruin my estates or make one of my tenants suffer."

"Such noble rage," he murmured. "No, my dear, my wants are simple. I have a desire to rusticate and sit in the country like a well-tended plant. You may go on as you have always gone on. You may handle the purse strings. According to the Marquis de Graux, you have been doing admirably since your husband's death. Why should I wish to kill the fat goose? I shall lie around your mansion like a comfortable old dog, content to be fed and petted from time to time."

His eyes began to close.

"Are you going to sleep at such a time?" demanded Delphine irritably.

His eyes flew open. "No. I must repair to my lodgings and collect my traps. Come with me. It is a sunny day, and we cannot sit here forever, circling around each other like two stray cats."

Delphine hesitated, and then nodded her head. She would need to spend the rest of her life with him. Better to get accustomed to him now. Once back at Marsham Manor, she would arrange a separate suite of rooms for him and retire into her old ways, and then she need not see him much.

And she had to admit reluctantly, although she still felt cheated, that he was infinitely pleasanter company than Mrs. Bencastle.

"We shall walk," said the comte, arranging his curly-brimmed beaver to a nicety on his fair hair.

He waited until Delphine had put on her bonnet again. Madame Beauchair's flat was on the first floor. It appeared she was lucky in having the whole floor to herself. The other French tenants in the building seemed to have only a room apiece.

The very warmth of the day felt foreign to Delphine as she walked through Manchester Square, listening to the sounds of French all about her. Previous springs had been hard and blustery, not warm and smiling like this one.

Arm in arm, they turned down Duke Street and onto Oxford Street. At the corner of Oxford Street, two ladies whose layers of paint were thicker than the muslin of their dresses turned at the approach of the newly married couple.

"Why, Monsoor Jules!" cried one. "Mr. Baxter was wondering where you had gone. You did not give him his French lesson."

"I am leaving for the country, Mrs. Baxter." The comte smiled. "I shall not be returning to London for some time."

"But you mustn't go away," wailed the one called Mrs. Baxter. "Whatever shall we do without you? We could raise your fees."

Delphine turned her head away and tried to look as if she were invisible.

"I'm afraid not," said Jules Saint-Pierre. "Good day to you."

Mrs. Baxter flashed Delphine a venomous, jealous glance.

This was to be the first of many such encounters on the couple's way to Soho. Fathers demanded to know why he had not called to give their children French lessons, two noisy bloods who leered at Delphine asked when he would be resuming his boxing lessons, and so it went on.

"I' faith," said the comte, tucking Delphine's hand more securely under his arm, "I should have *pretended* to resign before! Only see how they are prepared to raise their fees! Yet I charged little, fearing if I charged more that they would find someone else among the hundreds of French Londoners."

"You did not introduce me to any of these people," said Delphine severely.

"No, of course not," he replied equably. "It would be as good as saying 'See, I have married a rich wife so I no longer need your fees.' We have nearly arrived."

They walked through Soho Square and turned down a narrow cul-de-sac called Ramshorn's Court.

The comte was immediately besieged by children demanding entertainment.

"Not now." The comte smiled. "Later."

"There will be no 'later,'" said Delphine severely. "Now that you are married to me, I expect you to behave in a dignified manner."

"On second thought," called the comte to his audience of urchins, "I can spare you a few moments."

To Delphine's mortification, he began to juggle those wretched balls while the children cheered and clapped.

Her face flaming, she turned on her heel and marched away. She glanced over her shoulder, expecting the comte to cease his tomfoolery and run after her, but he did not pay her the slightest attention.

Delphine had just reached the corner of the street when she found her way barred by the small tiger she had seen with the comte at the fair.

"Ho! There you is, missus," he cried.

"Let me pass," said Delphine angrily. The tiger was not a boy at all. The bright sunlight revealed his face to be sharp and wrinkled. He was barely five feet high, which had led her to believe he was a child. His livery was exactly like the livery of a tiger, those minute individuals who acted as a sort of carriage-page to members of the ton. It was badly frayed and worn.

"You married Mister Jules, didn't you?" he demanded. "Well, you got to help him. There's a squad o' duns heading this way for to take him to the round'ouse."

Delphine stared at him, open-mouthed, and then whirled about and ran back towards the comte. She seized his arm and the colored balls went bouncing and spinning over the sun-drenched cobbles.

"Jules," she cried. "Your...your servant there says there are *duns* coming to see you."

"Quickly!" He put an arm around her waist and hustled her into the dark entry of a building nearby and ran up the steps two at a time. He took a key from his pocket, unlocked a door on the top landing, dragged her into a shabby room and locked the door, and leaned against it with his ear to the scarred panels.

"What on earth...?" began Delphine when she could catch her breath. "What are you *doing*?"

"Shhh!" he said, not moving a muscle.

"I shall *not* shush! I..."

He turned quickly and clamped his hand over her mouth. The physical contact aroused such a confused welter of emotions in her body that she could only stare up at him dumbly.

"I will take my hand away if you promise to whisper," he said in a voice which just reached her ears.

She nodded dumbly, and he took his hand away. "Have you any money?" he asked.

Delphine shook her head. "I have some money with my luggage in Manchester Square. But I shall refer your creditors to my lawyers..."

He looked her over and shook his head. "It would not serve," he said in a low voice. "They would not believe you a lady of substance. No jewels. No carriage. No maid."

"Then what shall we...?"

"Shhh! Don't let them know we are here, and perhaps they'll go away."

Thudding feet came rapidly up the stairs and the

next minute the door shook under heavy blows and kicks.

"Open up, Mr. Jules," cried one. "We know you're in there! Mrs. Jenkins told.us so."

"*Merde!*" said the comte.

"There is no need to swear," hissed Delphine, scarlet to the roots of her hair. "Who is Mrs. Jenkins?"

"Landlady."

"Break the door down," said a voice outside. "Macdonald here's got an axe."

"That does it!" said the comte. He picked up a leather wash bag and stuffed some papers in it. The room was barely furnished, containing only a narrow bed, a table, a rickety chair, and a washstand.

"Come," he said to Delphine. He went and gently eased up the window.

"Where are we going?" asked Delphine, stifling a scream as the first axe blow fell on the door.

"Over the roofs!"

"But I *can't*..."

He picked her up and tossed her over one shoulder and, doubling up with an acrobat's agility, gained the windowsill outside. Delphine stayed rigid across his shoulder. Far down below, the small mud-filled areas with their outside privies seemed miles away. She closed her eyes and gulped.

He seized the drainpipe and, still carrying her as if she weighed nothing at all, he shinnied up the drainpipe and then ran lightly over the sloping cracked tiles of the roof. One flying leap took him over to the roof of the building next door. There was no sound from Delphine. For the first time in her life, she had fainted dead away.

"Just as well," he muttered to himself.

He continued his headlong acrobatic flight from roof to roof until he reached the last one. He gently lowered Delphine down onto the roof with her back against a chimney stack and, working the string of her fan over her limp wrist until he got it free, he proceeded to fan her.

Delphine blinked up at him. Beyond his blue eyes stretched the blue of the sky. Down below...

She let out a sharp scream and clutched at his legs. He loosened her hold and eased himself down until he was sitting next to her.

"Don't say anything," he urged, "or you will be sick. Take deep breaths of air. *That's* the thing." Delphine did as she was bid, until the dizzy feeling of nausea passed. He put an arm around her shoulders and smiled down at her.

"We will wait here until they get tired and go away," he said.

"This is *monstrous*!" protested Delphine. She thought longingly of her dead husband, who had always treated her as if she were made of fragile porcelain.

Although he had encouraged her in the masculine study of agriculture, until his death that interest had been confined to gentle rides around the estates with him in his carriage. Sir George would *never* have subjected her to such peril. She glanced down, then closed her eyes.

"I wouldn't do that if you can't stand heights," said her husband sympathetically. "Some people can't, you know."

"You could have *killed* me," raged Delphine, fear being replaced by burning resentment and anger. "No *gentleman* would behave so."

"I think I have been very gentlemanly indeed," he said severely. "'T would not have been the act of a gentleman to allow you to suffer the indignities of the roundhouse. Now, instead, you are here with me, high above London on this sunny day. Over there you can see St. Paul's and beyond that, the Tower. There are not many places in London where you can find such a view. It's no use fretting about pride and dignity. All you will do is spoil our wedding day."

"Have you *no* realization of the outrageousness of your behavior, sirrah? Have you no shame?"

"I think I have been very resourceful," he said, picking up her fan and proceeding to fan her again. "You know, your eyes are beautiful when you are animated. Normally, they're sort of dead brown, like pennies, but when you take an interest in something, they sparkle with little lights, like a trout stream."

Delphine raised and dropped her hands in a gesture of resignation. "You're mad," she said. "Quite mad."

His arm about her shoulders made her wretched body all too aware of the proximity of his. She would have liked to move away from him, but there was really no safe place to move to.

"I have not had a real home in such a long time," he said reflectively. "Tell me about Marsham Manor. Tell me about the formidable Mrs. Bencastle."

At first, in the forced calm voice of someone trying to humor the mentally insane, Delphine obliged. But he listened so intently that she found herself talking more to him than she had talked to anyone in her life.

Gradually, she began to relax against his shoulder, talking and talking, while the sun gradually sank lower in the sky and the cheeky London sparrows squabbled in the gutters. She finished with a description of the marquis's visit and of how she had finally learnt of the manner of her parents' death.

"We all have such stories," he said. "Living with all the French *émigrés* has its advantages. One hears so many horrors that one's own seem to pale by comparison. Most of the poor things will not let the past go. For them, England is only an interlude."

"And for you?" asked Delphine curiously.

"Ah, for me, I tried to become as English as possible out of sheer contrariness. My outer shell is very English, but my soul is French. Look! There is going to be a new moon tonight and the first star is out. Soon we may go."

"Since you seem to have had so many occupations," said Delphine, "why are you in such straits? Why cannot you pay your creditors?"

"It was my wretched vanity, my sweeting. I was determined to pay for the wedding breakfast and to have a new suit of clothes. But before I could pay my tailor or my rent or my coffee house bills or my bootmaker, I unfortunately felt obliged to give money to some needy friends, and so..."

"You are irresponsible," said Delphine. "Such conduct must change."

"I will be *very* good," he said solemnly. "I am much too lazy to go against your wishes."

Delphine bit her lip in vexation. Somehow, he managed to make her feel like a boring and nagging middle-aged matron.

But she had quite forgotten about the perils of the descent still awaiting her until he cocked an ear, listened to the noises of the street below, and said, "It is time to go now."

"Oh, no!" wailed Delphine, beginning to tremble.

He stood up and raised her to her feet. He steadied himself with one hand on the chimney stack, seeing the glint of fear in her wide eyes.

The comte suddenly bent his head and kissed her ferociously, passionately, his lips moving against her own. Delphine tried to resist him, but she felt her body melting into his, and the stars and moon above began to whirl and spin.

He suddenly released her, only to swing her over his shoulder, leaving her too dazed and shaken by that kiss to protest or utter a sound.

The man is like a cat! she thought as he nimbly scaled down the drainpipe of the last house and, still holding her, ran across a small, odorous yard, leapt onto a barrel and was over a wall, jumping from the top and landing on the other side without a sound.

He set her on her feet and, tucking her hand in his

arm, set off sedately through Soho Square with the stately tread of a bourgeois gentleman out for a Sunday walk with his wife.

Delphine stumbled from time to time, weary with emotion and fatigue, but his hand was always there to steady her. Several times, she opened her mouth to say something and closed it again.

At last, the corner of Manchester Square was reached. A small shadow detached itself from the blacker shadow of a building. "Guv," it whispered hoarsely.

"Yes, Charlie, what's amiss?" asked the comte.

"I wus wonderin' whether you was going wiffout sayin' good-bye."

"No, I wouldn't dream of it, and my dear wife will not object, I am sure, to my taking my only servant with me."

The little man squinted up at Delphine, trying to see her face in the dark. "Have you got horses, missus?" he asked. "*Real* horses?"

"Yes, real horses," said Delphine wearily. What on earth were her aged servants going to make of Charlie?

"It's a long time since me and the guv had one," he said plaintively.

"We are residing at Madame Beauchair's, Charlie," said the comte firmly. "Come and see me in the morning."

The small man touched his hat and scuttled off into the darkness.

"He has been with me almost since I came to this country," explained the comte. "I had a certain amount of my family's jewels with me, then. I did not dare try to sell them in France, since I was masquerading as a peasant boy during my escape. But in London ... Well, I was very young and thought I had a fortune. The money from the jewels did not last very long, and so, bit by bit, everything went, until finally I had only one horse and then that had to go, too. But Charlie stayed. He was my tiger and hopes to be so again."

Madame Beauchair's flat looked slightly more welcoming than it had earlier, with the soft candlelight masking the shabbiness of the furniture.

A cold supper had been left for them. Obviously Madame Beauchair's maid had gone to join her mistress.

After a little hesitation, Delphine went into the bedroom to change, leaving her husband to open the wine.

She selected a plain morning gown, not wanting to wear evening dress, since her husband now had only the clothes he stood up in.

She washed and changed quickly. Her gown was of plain cambric, high at the neck and let in around the bottom with two rows of worked trimming. It was pale blue with darker blue embroidery.

Her husband surveyed her with a critical eye as he drew out a chair for her. "Not blue," he said finally. "With your skin and hair, you should wear more dramatic colors, scarlet or burgundy, I think."

Delphine unrolled her hapkin and glanced up at him with irritation. "My dear sir, I am at least neat and clean. You have all the dirt of the London roofs about your person."

"I know," he rejoined. "I must spend my wedding night washing my clothes."

There came a loud knocking at the door. The comte instinctively glanced towards the window.

"No," said Delphine firmly. "I am not going to run over any more roofs. I have money here." She marched to the door and opened it, prepared to face a battalion of duns.

But it was only the small figure of the tiger. "I got the guvner's traps, missus," he said, touching a battered and shiny excuse for a hat with one finger.

The comte came to join Delphine. "Wonderful, Charlie," he said. "How did you manage it?"

"I waited till that old horse godmother, Mrs. Jenkins, took herself off for her quart o' blue ruin and jemmied the lock an' snaffled 'em."

He touched his hat again and prepared to withdraw.

"Wait," said Delphine. She ran into the bedroom and returned a few moments later and handed Charlie several gold coins.

"Pray find yourself a suitable livery on the morrow," said Delphine. "I understand you are to accompany your master and me to Marsham Manor."

Charlie looked from Delphine to the gold. Then he slid it into one of the many pockets in his ragged coat, mumbled "yes missus" and darted off down the stairs, leaving his master's trunks on the landing.

The comte lifted them inside the room and waved a hand towards the table. "Come, *ma cherie*, we must eat."

Now, Delphine was not used to being criticized, except by Mrs. Bencastle. Sir George would not have dreamed of finding fault with her dress. She whipped open her napkin again with a noise like a flag flapping in the wind and studied her husband.

"You seem to set yourself up in matters of dress," she said coldly while he carved a ham into delicate slivers. "No doubt you have much experience in such matters."

He smiled at her vaguely but did not reply.

Delphine was tired. She found herself becoming increasingly irritated. "No doubt you learned about ladies' fashions from the wives of your clients," she pursued. "They seemed monstrous upset to find you were leaving for the country."

"Yes," he said equably. "I was a prime favorite."

"I trust you confined your instructions to the drawing room?"

"Oh, no." He smiled sleepily. "I gave great service in the bedroom as well."

"Shameless! How dare..."

"Mr. Baxter often said no one could instruct a man to tie a cravat like me."

Delphine blushed. "It pleases you to make fun of me," she said in a low voice.

"I? I was merely answering your questions. Do eat. You have no idea how spleenish one can become when one is hungry."

"I am *not* spleenish!"

"But you are hungry."

"Not at all."

"Then I hope you will not mind if *I* eat. I confess to feeling very sharp-set."

Delphine watched with lowered eyes as he heaped his plate and set to with a will. He ate slowly, neatly, and fastidiously. He appeared to have his mind solely on his food.

The candles on the small round table at which they were seated were now the only ones lit. He must have extinguished the others while she was dressing, thought Delphine.

The tall candles on the table isolated them in a golden pool of light. She scowled at her plate and waited for him to say something so that she could contradict him. But he continued to help himself from the cold collation that had been left for them.

Her stomach gave a treacherous rumble. Slowly, Delphine picked up her knife and fork. She would just eat a very little. But no sooner had she finished the first mouthful than she realized how ravenously hungry she was. The meat—ham, veal, and cold game pie— was delicious. It had been cooked to perfection, each piece having a delicate, subtle flavor quite unlike any of the dishes at Marsham Manor.

All at once, her hunger appeased, Delphine began to feel ashamed of herself, and wondered at her behavior. She could not remember having ever behaved in such a *pettish* fashion in her life.

But her feeling of well-being did not last long.

She realized her anger at him had stopped her for a short time from remembering that they were married and that there was only one bedroom and only one bed.

Delphine began to feel exhausted, nervous, and on the point of tears. He seemed so large, so very tall, and he had kissed her in that shocking way. What if he should kiss her again?

She was aware of his eyes on her downcast face. "Go to bed," he said gently. "I am used to being my own servant and am quite capable of tidying things here."

Delphine arose slowly, still not looking at him, and scurried from the room.

She undressed in frantic haste, terrified he would walk in and surprise her. She scrambled into her nightgown and tied a nightcap on top of her hair.

The bed was a large four-poster with worn brocade hangings. The sheets were thin and cold and smelled of lavender.

Delphine snuggled down and lay rigid, wondering what he was going to do.

Chapter Four

❖

She awoke in the morning, lying in exactly the same position as she had when she fell asleep. All the cries of London assailed her ears from below the windows. Sunlight dappled the bed, shining through the worn patches in the brocade curtains.

Delphine closed her eyes again and tried to escape back down the corridors of sleep, away from the thoughts of her marriage and the dread of returning to Marsham Manor and of seeing Maria Bencastle's face.

But someone was selling lavender, someone was determined that the whole of London should awake and buy her lavender. The voice screeched abominably like a rusty farm gate.

And then Delphine became aware she was not alone in the bed.

She struggled up against the pillows and looked down at her husband.

He was sleeping, neatly and quietly on his side.

His hair under his red nightcap was tousled. His face looked closed, secretive. What did she really know of him? thought Delphine in sudden panic.

She decided to dress quickly and go and see her lawyers by herself. They would be shocked enough by the step she had taken. But what if she took her husband along and he started juggling balls or balancing plates?

Besides, she desperately needed to escape from the intimacy of this situation. She longed to be alone.

Since Sir George had never favored the social life, Delphine had somehow never used the services of a lady's maid, contenting herself by making most of her own clothes and arranging her own hair in simple styles.

She was used to going about the countryside on her own. There could be little difference in traveling about London unescorted.

It was only when she was finally walking out of the square, desperately trying to find a hack, that she began to lose heart. An aged Jehu spat in her direction and continued on his way, his broken-down hackney carriage making a tremendous noise as it lurched over the cobbles.

It seemed as if the hackney drivers of London did not favor single women.

And then a party of bloods came roistering drunkenly down the street. They had obviously been carousing all night.

They saw Delphine, took in her appearance from her modest dress to her fashionable bonnet. They whispered among themselves, and, as they came abreast of her, they unflapped their breeches and began to make water against the railings, tittering and sniggering, avidly watching her face for her reaction.

Delphine picked up her heels and fled down Duke Street, followed by a volley of jeering cackles.

Then she heard them starting up in pursuit. There

is nothing your London buck loves more than the discomfiture of a gently bred miss.

It was then that Delphine recognized the diminutive figure of her husband's tiger coming towards her. He, too, had obviously been celebrating. His gait was none too steady, and he had a knot of pink ribbons pinned at the side of his reprehensible hat.

There were new wine stains on his tattered blue plush livery with its ragged ghosts of epaulettes on each shoulder.

He had a large parcel under one arm.

"Morning, missus," he said cheerfully. "Got me livery, just like you said."

The sound of London's aristocracy baying for the sight of a maidenly blush came closer.

"Charlie!" exclaimed Delphine in despair. "These gentlemen are pestering me, and I must find a hack and get to my lawyers."

Charlie nipped around Delphine with surprising speed and faced her tormenters. He berated them in a cant so mercifully broad that it was impossible for Delphine to understand a word. Her tormenters tried to retaliate, but it appeared that Charlie was a past master in the art of abuse, and soon she found they had stumbled past and she was left in peace.

"Now, missus," said Charlie, coming closer to her. Delphine took a quick step back to escape the fumes of last night's wine and heavily spiced food. "'Ave you got money or 'aven't you?"

"You are presumptuous," replied Delphine coldly. "Go about your business."

"An' leave you alone? Naaah! The guv wouldn't like it. Shouldn't 'ave come out wiffout him. Up to every rig and row in town, the guvner is."

Delphine raised her chin and tried to walk on.

"Look'ee here, missus," said Charlie, blocking her way. His voice seesawed between pure cockney and a ridiculous parody of his master's upper-class drawl.

"It's a practical question. Ladies wiff money don't go abaht calling hacks. There's a livery stable close by. I can git you a slap-up turnout fer the day, coachman and all. Go to your lawyers in style."

Pride warred with common sense in Delphine's breast. Common sense won.

"Very well," she said. "Lead the way."

Delphine had to admit that the disgraceful Charlie was a great comfort. In no time at all, it seemed, she was seated in a smart carriage pulled by two spanking horses.

Charlie was perched on the backstrap with a blissful expression on his face. It was an open carriage, and so she was able to relax and watch the sights of London as they made their way down Oxford Street in the direction of the City.

"Told the guv where you was goin', missus?" called Charlie at one point.

Delphine shook her head.

"He'll think you've broken your shackles. Left him a note, did you?"

Delphine fought down a desire to tell Charlie to "know his place." "No, I did not think it necessary," she said.

"Bad, that," said the tiger reflectively. "He won't be there when we get back."

"Why on earth not?" demanded Delphine.

"What man would?" replied the tiger.

Delphine twisted her head around and looked at him in surprise, but the tiger had seen a shabby acquaintance in the street and was now showing off to the top of his bent, sitting bolt upright, his hands folded across his chest and his hat tipped at a cocky angle.

Delphine turned back. She wondered how she would feel if this new husband of hers had indeed taken himself off. Relieved, she told herself firmly. The whole thing has been a terrible mistake. Yes, thought Delphine, I should be *very* relieved.

* * *

The Comte Saint-Pierre stretched lazily in bed, remembered his wedding, and stretched out one arm. Finding he was alone in the bed, he sleepily swung his long legs out onto the floor, rubbed his eyes, and stared about the room.

He wondered whether to go and look for his wife while wearing only his nightshirt and decided against it.

There was a clattering of dishes and a smell of coffee from the kitchen, which was on the other side of the living room. That must be Delphine, making breakfast.

He had begun to have several sharp and nagging doubts about the wisdom of this marriage the previous evening, but the sounds of this wifely chore made him smile.

He thought of Delphine's wide eyes, chestnut hair, and trim figure and began to feel happy.

Whistling cheerfully, he washed himself thoroughly at the washstand and dressed with care, noticing with pleasure that he had managed to remove all traces of his flight across the roofs from his new coat and breeches. There were a few scratches on his new Hessians, but if you have been wearing ones that are patched and mended for quite some time, as the comte had been, a few scratches on a new pair seemed of little matter.

He tied his cravat in the Mathematical, straightened his waistcoat, and, still whistling cheerfully, went off to join his wife for breakfast.

The whistle died on his lips and the smile died from his eyes as he found only the red-handed waif busy in the kitchen.

"Where is her ladyship?" he asked, leaning against the doorjamb.

Although the maid, who was called Marie, had been addressed by him in French, she had always been firmly convinced he was English and essayed to reply to him in that difficult language.

"Gone," was all she finally managed.

"Gone where, Marie?"

"Do not know, milord."

The comte wheeled about and went back to the bedroom and looked thoughtfully at his wife's trunk, which had still not been unpacked although she had obviously extracted several garments from it that morning.

His eye fell on the lowboy in the corner of the room. Neatly stacked on top was a small pile of golden guineas.

He poked at them with one long finger, an expression of distaste crossing his face. He knew Delphine had left the money for him, therefore it followed logically that Delphine had gone. She could afford to abandon the few clothes she had brought with her.

He walked slowly back to the kitchen and silently collected a tray with coffee and brioches from the maid.

The vision of a charming Delphine was rapidly fading from his mind, to be replaced by a picture of a querulous and fault-finding Delphine.

The comte ate his breakfast mechanically, half wondering why he felt so bitter.

He had received many slights and snubs during his London career so he could not quite understand why he should feel such a mixture of sadness and resentment.

A knock at the door roused him from his reverie, but he allowed the maid to answer it.

He suppressed a groan as Madame de Manton bustled into the room. Madame de Manton was a middle-aged lady of ferocious energy. She had large, innocent gray eyes in a rouged and painted face. Her thin, wiry figure was briefly covered in the gauziest of muslin gowns, and her hennaed curls peeped out from beneath an enormous bonnet with a whole flower garden on top.

Madame de Manton had only last week relieved him of the few guineas he had saved for his wedding finery. She was an inveterate gambler and always on the point of being dragged off to the nearest debtor's prison.

"Where is the comtesse?" she asked in French, peering around the room and then at the floor, as if expecting to find Delphine under the furniture.

"Gone out on business," said the comte laconically. "You are looking very fine, madame. I trust you paid your debts before you bought that ravishing gown."

"I have. But better than that! I am come to repay you." Triumphantly Madame de Manton put a rouleau of guineas on the table. "There was this horse running at Newmarket..."

The comte groaned and covered his face with his hands.

"No, *chéri*. It was Providence!" cried Madame, tugging his hands away from his face.

"I was about to pay my debts with the money you gave me when Armand Duclos told me he was going to Newmarket and there was this horse running called Lucky Peter. Now, Peter is English for Pierre and since you are *very* lucky, I thought, why not? I won a *lot* of money on Lucky Peter and was about to leave when what should I find in the next race but a horse called Marriage Vow! Do not groan in that silly way. It won! So here is not only the money you gave me the last time, but the time before and the time before.

"I had hoped to find your wife with you. It is your wedding morn...?"

"The English are not sentimental about such things," said the comte dryly.

"*Vraiment*! How very odd. You see, an English friend, Mrs. Brandenbaugh, is giving a breakfast at her home at Richmond which commences at three this afternoon. I have hired a carriage and I thought it would be pleasant for you and your wife to accompany me. Such a beautiful day!"

The comte picked up his coffee cup and gazed straight ahead. Even in sooty, noisy London, he could hear the twittering and chattering of birds. It promised to be that English rarity, an extremely warm spring day. It would be irritating and embarrassing to stay in this dark apartment waiting for a wife he was sure would not return. Had she not gone out of her way to show him that she thought the marriage was a dreadful mistake?

He had worked so long and so hard. It seemed ages since he had had any fun. It seemed years since he had looked at a woman.

Lying celibate next to Delphine's slim, rounded body had given him a long and sleepless night, and he had only managed to close his eyes shortly before dawn.

He wanted to look at pretty women, flirt with them a little, and get mildly drunk. There would be other callers, friends in the French community coming to pay their respects to the new bride. It would be embarrassing to stay.

The comte made up his mind. "My wife has gone to see her lawyers on business," he said slowly, although privately he believed Delphine to be well on her way to Bedfordshire.

"She will be away for most of the day and the early evening as well. I will come with you." He looked at the clock. It was half past eleven. "I shall call for you at twelve-thirty, in an hour's time."

"Wonderful!" said Madame de Manton. "We will send the carriage back to fetch your wife. Is it not amazing that the English should call something a 'breakfast' which begins at three in the afternoon and goes on all night?"

"I will leave her a note," said the comte. "My wife has her own carriage," he added, sure that Delphine had hired a carriage to take her home. He had no intention of leaving a note for a wife who would never see it.

"Of course. It will be wonderful to meet her. I knew Félice, her mother, very well. What a charming, gay, and lighthearted woman she was! I suppose her daughter is the same?"

The comte did not reply.

"Ah, well. *À bientôt.*" Madame departed in a flutter of muslin, leaving the comte alone. The servant, Marie, was doing mysterious things in the kitchen. No doubt Madame Beauchair would be the next to arrive.

With an impatient movement, he rose from the table and quit the apartment, snatching up the rouleau of guineas as he did so.

Delphine spent a long, hot, and dusty time with her lawyers getting nowhere. All she seemed to do was listen to their wailings and protests over "this ill-advised marriage." Then she went to her bank to explain the change in her circumstances and name. Reluctant to return to Manchester Square, she decided to visit the Tower and see the menagerie. Charlie, torn between running back to Manchester Square to explain to his master what Delphine was doing and a burning desire to see the wild beasts at the Tower, finally settled for the Tower, comforting his conscience with the thought that the comte would never forgive him should anything happen to his wife, and also comforting himself with a shrewd thought that his master would certainly not be waiting for his wife to deign to return.

Charlie knew the stubborn streak of pride which lurked under his master's easy-going exterior, better than the comte knew it himself. And Charlie knew that whether the comte did not want to see his wife again was beside the point. The comte still would not forgive him if he abandoned Delphine to the tender mercies of the London streets.

So Charlie enjoyed his day much more than Delphine. Delphine was beginning to be plagued with a nagging feeling that she was behaving badly.

Had not the comte suggested he would be happy to have the marriage annulled if that was what she wished?

But it was five o'clock in the afternoon before they finally returned to Manchester Square, the Tower of London being much farther from the West End than Delphine thought it was.

"He won't be home," said Charlie.

Delphine refused to reply. But when she walked into the flat and found it deserted, she experienced a stab of fear. What if the duns had found him? How would she ever find out? Then she relaxed. Charlie would know.

"His traps are gone," said Charlie, who had walked into the bedroom without so much as a by-your-leave. "And you didn't tell him where you was going. Probably he thought you left him."

"Why on earth should he think that?" demanded Delphine crossly, her curiosity overcoming her desire to give this insolent tiger the setdown he was obviously so badly in need of.

"I watched you coming out of the wedding," said Charlie. "Face like a fiddle, beggin' your parding, I'm sure. Looked as though you couldn't stand the sight of him, that you did, and he noticed it, 'e did. I knows him, see. Then you ups and orfs on your wedding morn, leaving money for him like he was a demy-rep."

"And where is this wounded and cut-to-the-quick master of yours now, think you?" demanded Delphine.

"Probly as drunk as David's sow, missus. I can see 'im a-lyin' on some boozing ken floor with his heart broke."

"Fiddle!" snapped Delphine. She was beginning to feel guilty and, like most guilty people, she changed the feeling promptly into one of justified anger.

"It is not my fault," she said and then bit her lip.

What had come over her that she should start apologizing to a shabby servant?

Charlie knew he had gone too far and immediately presented a picture of abject subservience, although he watched her face from under his stubby eyelashes.

"Where do you think he is?"

"Don't know, my lady," said Charlie, according her her title for the first time. "Ain't that servant abaht?"

But Marie had obviously only been there for a short time before returning to her mistress. The living room was clean, and the fire made up.

Delphine shook her head.

"I can find out," said Charlie after some thought. "T'ain't hard to find out fings in this area."

He darted off. Delphine sat down on a spindly chair and wondered what to do.

It was too late to secure a seat on the mail coach. She could always hire a carriage, but that would mean a journey through the night, facing the perils of highwaymen and footpads.

Her nagging conscience was telling her she hadn't even given this odd marriage a chance. Someone was singing in French in the square outside, his song punctuated by giggles from a female audience. Delphine lit the candles to banish the darkness, which was gathering in the room.

Her eyes fell on a small shelf of French books. She took out a novel and settled down to read, willing herself to concentrate on the words.

An hour passed and still Charlie did not return.

Perhaps he had found out the whereabouts of his master, and both were sitting in some low coffee house or tavern toasting the comte's escape from this marriage of convenience.

All at once, there came an excited hammering on the door. Delphine went to answer it.

"He's gone to a breakfast in Richmond," said Charlie cheerfully. "At a Mrs. Brandenbaugh. I have the direction. I've got a carriage outside and grooms an' all, belongs to a Monsoor Duclos. It'll take us there, quick as quick."

"I do not wish to go where I am not wanted," said Delphine stiffly.

"Oo says you wasn't wanted, missus?" demanded Charlie in pained tones. "Seems to me like the guv thought *he* wasn't wanted. Might as least go along and say hullo."

Delphine thought hard, pride warring with guilt. Then her eye fell on a tray of cards on a table near the door, and she silently turned them over. The Marquis de Graux and Monsieur Renaud had called. So had many others of the French community.

"I've got me new livery," pleaded Charlie. "I could change in the kitching. Don't want to sport your blunt on a new livery, missus, and never let it see the light o' day."

"Oh, very well," said Delphine crossly. "Wait for me. I must change."

Alone in the bedroom, Delphine unfolded a gown from its tissue paper. She had made it during the winter in the faint hope that one day she might go to a ball. The dress was a beautiful specimen of silver embroidery on the sheerest mull, and it was to be worn over a slip of white satin. She had copied it from an illustration in *La Belle Assemblée*. Quickly she washed and changed and put it on. Over it she wore a pelisse of cambric, called a "fugitive coat," trimmed with Vandyke edging and embroidery.

She brushed her hair until it shone and arranged it in a Grecian style, pinning two large white silk roses among her glossy curls.

Roman pearl drop earrings, a silver fan, and white linen gloves completed the ensemble.

When she entered the living room, Charlie was already strutting about in his new livery.

His coat was a tight little scarlet tunic like a jockey's, decorated with three rows of steel buttons. He had buckskin smallclothes, top boots, and an old-fashioned three-cornered hat with a white cockade stuck in it. He told Delphine later that it had once belonged to a noble supporter of Bonnie Prince Charlie who had lost his head on the Tower block, and the executioner had popped the deceased's hat at the pawn.

Under his hat, he wore a white wig which had been designed for a larger head than Charlie's. His small, dirty face was shadowed by the enormous front curls, but Charlie seemed to think it his crowning glory.

Monsieur Duclos's coach was a great state affair, encrusted with flaking gold paint. The seats inside were spilling their stuffing onto the floor, and Delphine had to sit on a blanket to protect herself from the prickly horsehair which stuck out of the rents in the upholstery.

Charlie was in seventh heaven. Sometimes little groups of people would set up a ragged cheer as the great coach dipped and swayed and rumbled past.

In the dim light from the dirty parish lamps, Monsieur Duclos's coach did look rather like one of the royal carriages.

Delphine began to wonder what on earth her husband would do and say when he saw her.

The Comte Saint-Pierre was relieved to find that Madame de Manton was the only member of his compatriots at the breakfast. He did not wish to be asked about his marriage or to answer questions about his wife.

He had been a success, particularly with the ladies. To them, he was an unattached and handsome man. With his usual finesse, he had avoided the debutantes and settled on the company of his hostess, Mrs. Brandenbaugh, a merry widow of uncertain years. She had faded blue eyes and a pale aureole of golden hair, almost too gold. She had painted her face with the hand of an artist.

She had lost none of the coquetry of her youth, nor had she lost her excellent full-breasted figure whose charms were daringly revealed by the damped gold tissue of her gown.

His wounded pride appreciated each pressure of her hand and each roguish glance from her eyes. He had often, in the past, had the opportunity to become some wealthy lady's cicisbeo and settle down to a lapdog life of comparative ease until his wrinkles put him out of favor. But he had valued his independence. He was proud of his name and his family. Unlike many of the other French *émigrés*, he had no dream of his lands being restored. He had been content to work hard and enjoy himself as much as possible. His skill in juggling and conjuring had been parlor games during his childhood to amuse his parents and their friends. In his years in London, they had often been his sole means of livelihood.

When Madame Beauchair had run up to him at the fair, gasping that she had seen the ghost of Félice de Fleuris, he had thought it one of her many fancies. So many of them had had their brains slightly addled by the horrors they had seen.

But when it had transpired that the pretty, vivacious young woman who had given him a guinea was none other than his betrothed, he had felt a quickening of the senses and the beginnings of hope.

Jules Saint-Pierre had had many affairs, most of them light and pleasant, but he had never been in love.

He was very much his parents' son. Love did not enter into marriage. A suitable alliance was contracted between your own family and that of another, and you were honor-bound to abide by your parents' wishes.

Had Delphine had no money, he would have wished to marry her just the same. He had a craving to put down roots and form some sort of family; to have children to carry on his name. But the fact that she was very wealthy indeed did have added charms; that much he had to admit. To once again own lands and belong somewhere seemed like the fulfillment of a dream.

But he had not taken into account the character of the woman he was to marry.

She was, at times, rude, silent, gauche, willful, and, at others, charming beyond belief.

Not at all the complaisant female he had imagined.

Well, it was over now. That much she had shown by leaving him in such a cavalier fashion, by leaving money for him.

He wondered what she was doing.

And poor Charlie, who dreamed from morning till night of horses, nothing but horses, and who had stuck loyally to his penniless master. Would Charlie be content to return to the old ways?

There was dancing and food and music and cards, noise and laughter all about. Mrs. Brandenbaugh squeezed past him in the press, leaning against him deliberately so that he could feel the pressure of her full breasts against his back and smell the musk of her perfume.

He gave a little sigh and turned and put his hands at her waist and smiled down into her eyes.

"Why don't you show me these famous gardens of yours?" he teased. "'Tis suffocating in here."

Mrs. Brandenbaugh gave a nervous giggle but led the way through long french windows and out onto a terrace overlooking the gardens.

Formal bushes and trees, grass, and flowers stretched out in the light from the house and disappeared into the blackness. For a moment, he forgot about Mrs. Brandenbaugh and willed himself back to his father's château on the Loire, looking down at the sleepy curves of the river and the jumble of pointed roofs of the village, which huddled against the walls of the castle.

He could almost smell the thyme and rosemary from his mother's herb garden. He half closed his eyes, seeing again the sunlight on the flat fields bordering the Loire while over in the distance rose the turrets and battlements of the de Fleuris château.

"Dreaming?" teased a light voice at his elbow.

He gave a little shrug and smiled lazily down at Mrs. Brandenbaugh. "Dreaming of you, ma'am," he said. All he had to do was put an arm around her waist and draw her close and it would be understood that he could stay the night after the other guests had gone. All he had to do was finally admit to himself that his strange marriage had been a mistake.

She swayed towards him slightly, her lips parted and her eyes bright.

He bent his head very slowly towards her.

"What is it, James?"

The comte blinked. A footman was standing nervously, holding a card on a tray.

"A lady to see the Comte Saint-Pierre," said the footman, staring into the middle distance and holding out the tray.

Mrs. Brandenbaugh snatched the card. "One of your admirers in full pursuit?" She peered at the card, holding it up to the light shining from the window.

Mrs. Brandenbaugh's gaze flew from the card to the comte's face. He twitched the card from her fingers and, taking out his quizzing glass, studied the inscription.

"Lady Charteris" had been scored out and printed neatly underneath was "The Comtesse Saint-Pierre."

"Your sister?" queried his hostess faintly.

He had only to tell her he had no wife or sister. He had only to tell her he had never heard of the Comtesse Saint-Pierre and Delphine would be sent on her way.

But she had followed him all the way from London...

"My wife," he said.

"Your *wife*? I was not aware you were married."

"I was married yesterday."

"It is cold outside," said Mrs. Brandenbaugh in a thin voice. Without looking at the comte again, she walked off down the terrace, her head held high.

The comte turned to the footman. "Lead the way."

Delphine was sitting in an anteroom off the main hall, her reticule on her lap, back straight, knees together, looking straight ahead, a faint tinge of embarrassment coloring her cheeks.

The comte closed the door behind him and leaned his broad shoulders against it and studied his bride, noting the glittering, elaborate gown and the glossy curls.

"I am honored," he said, walking forward and raising her hand to his lips.

She snatched her hand away and buried it in her lap.

"Very well," he said quietly. "Why did you come?"

"To see you," she replied in an odd, rusty sort of voice.

"And now you have seen me...?"

"I don't know," she said miserably. "You went away without telling me where you were going."

"As you did not? You said the day before that *we*—*we*, mark you—would go to your lawyers."

"I decided to go alone."

"Why?"

"I thought they would be shocked enough without actually meeting you."

"You are rude."

"I mean, I thought you might start juggling things and producing rabbits from hats."

"In short, you are ashamed of me."

Delphine thought desperately, and then said in a small voice, "Yes."

"Then there is no more to be said. You will find the money you left me untouched. May I suggest we tear

71

up our marriage lines and forget about the whole unfortunate episode?"

"We gave our oaths before God..."

"To love and to cherish? I see little of *that* in your behavior."

Delphine remained silent.

"So," he said at last, "I will escort you to town and wave farewell to you on the morrow and then return to my reprehensible pursuits."

"Very well," snapped Delphine. She did not know what she had expected of him. A little gratitude perhaps? She could not really believe that he was throwing her fortune away. She cast a fleeting glance at his face. He was stifling a yawn.

"Are you *always* sleepy?" she demanded.

"Always," he said amiably.

They made their good-byes to their hostess, who looked scornfully at Delphine and pleadingly at the comte.

Delphine caught the glance. It was brought home to her for the first time that the comte had not needed to marry her if he wished to marry money.

Outside, Charlie, a huge grin stretching from ear to ear, was holding open the carriage door, bowing so low he seemed likely to split his new buckskins.

"Dear me, Charlie," said the comte, surveying his servant's new finery. "In good coat, I see!"

He helped Delphine into the cumbersome coach and then settled himself beside her.

He pulled a dusty carriage rug over her legs and an antiquated bearskin over his own.

The coach rumbled forward.

The comte closed his eyes and went to sleep.

So that was that, thought Delphine as the coach rumbled down the tree-lined drive.

Tears pricked at the back of her lids, and she felt rejected and very much alone.

Somehow she had pictured him being delighted to

see her, reassured, and glad that she had not left him after all.

She stole a look at him. He was very handsome. Many women must find him so. Women who wore scandalous gowns like Mrs. Brandenbaugh; scented, frivolous women, not timid country mice like herself.

She had never wondered about her own attractions. Sir George had adored her. But he had encouraged her to share his isolated life. Faintly from behind them came the strains of a waltz.

"I thought I might have a chance to dance," thought Delphine miserably.

She took a handkerchief out of her reticule and blew her nose hard.

A rising wind rattled the branches of the trees on the right of the road and sent ripples scurrying across the surface of the river on her left.

Nothing lay before her now but a return to the old ways, to rustic stagnation with only the sound of Maria Bencastle's carping to ruffle the still waters of her life, the way the wind was ruffling the water of the river.

The coach slowed as it started to ascend the crest of an old hump-backed bridge. How near the water looked!

The coach gave a lurch. The horses reared and neighed. The comte opened one eye and raised one sleepy eyebrow.

Out in the darkness of the Richmond night, a great voice cried, "Stand and deliver!"

Chapter Five

❦

Delphine let out a scream.

"*Quiet!*" said the comte. "They kill their victims on this road, as I recall."

He opened the carriage door beside Delphine. She found herself looking at a low parapet with the river shining in the moonlight underneath. The River Thames looked swift and fast and deadly.

"Out!" whispered the comte. "Beside me. On the parapet."

Delphine was too shocked to do anything other than obey him.

The carriage door on the far side was wrenched open, and a masked face peered in.

The comte, balanced on the parapet with his arm around Delphine's waist, suddenly dived headlong into the river, taking her with him.

They plunged down into the icy water, down and down and down, until Delphine felt they could never manage to rise again. Then the comte began to pull her up towards the surface. She felt her lungs would burst. Just when it seemed the roaring, pounding, suffocating nightmare of the icy water would go on forever, her head broke above the surface of the water, and she took a gasping breath of air.

"Don't thrash or struggle," said her husband's calm voice in her ear. "Let me hold you."

Delphine shook the water from her eyes. One of the roses dropped from her wet hair and went spinning off down the river.

The moon had come out. The black bulk of the coach could just be seen, lumbering off in the distance, swinging around the turn in the road which would take it away from the river.

On the bridge stood two black, masked figures. There was a flash of light, and a bullet spat into the water near Delphine's head.

"Down again," said the comte cheerfully.

Delphine took in a huge breath of air just in time. The next second, he had doubled over and dived, still holding her firmly, dragging her back down into those terrifying, roaring depths of the river.

"This is it!" thought Delphine in a confused, panicky way. "This is death. How stupid!"

Her senses began to swim. She could not possibly hold her breath any longer. Then she began to feel herself being pulled back up.

Again, her head broke the surface, and the watery moon and stars wheeled above the rushing river.

They were close to the brush and undergrowth of a small island.

"Put your arms around my neck," said the comte in a low voice, "and don't make a sound. Voices carry easily on the water."

Numbly, she did as she was bid. He swam with strong steady strokes around the island so that they were on the far side of it, away from the bridge.

75

There was a small pebbly beach, gleaming white in the moonlight. They crawled up it on their hands and knees. Delphine was shivering uncontrollably.

"Wait here," said the comte. He moved off across the little island, creeping silently from tree to tree. Silence fell, broken only by the sounds of the river.

After what seemed an age, he came silently back. "They've gone," he said cheerfully.

"Are you *mad*?" demanded Delphine through chattering teeth. "You nearly drowned me. I have money with me! We could have given it to them, and then they would have let us go on our way."

"Not these men," he said. "I had forgotten until they held us up. There have been reports of two highwaymen on the Richmond road who *enjoy* killing their victims. Why do you think they let the coach go? Why do you think they stayed, risking capture, in order to shoot at us in the water? Charlie, the grooms, and the coachman survived because these men are only interested in killing the rich, not their servants. That tawdry coach of Duclos looks like the carriage of a very rich aristocrat in the darkness."

Sitting on the beach, Delphine hugged her knees and tried to control her shivering.

"In any case," he said, "we may as well swim to shore."

"What!" screamed Delphine. "No! I am not going back in that water again."

"Then wait here," he said with unruffled good humor, "and I will swim to shore and find a boat."

There was a sharp crackle in the undergrowth as some nocturnal animal made its rounds.

Delphine started. "No! Don't leave me," she pleaded. "What if the highwaymen have found a boat and come looking for me?"

"I don't think they will," he said. "Never mind, we will wait until morning. Now, I should have my tinderbox somewhere. If we can have a fire. . . . Ah, here it is."

He gathered up dry ferns and brush and piled them up. "Now let us see if I can get a spark from this poor, wet device."

Delphine sat and watched him as he patiently tried to light the fire. She had almost stopped shivering as an all-consuming rage engulfed her.

Never had she been treated thus!

"You do not seem particularly worried about my health, sir," she said, between chattering teeth.

He looked at her with infuriating calm. "No, I think you will survive," he said reasonably.

"You forget, I am a gently bred lady and not some doxy who lives on the streets!"

"I was told by the Marquis de Graux," he said, "that you worked hard and rode out in all weathers. I was most impressed. I must remind you again, furthermore, that we have not all been as fortunate as Delphine de Fleuris, and most of us have had to live lives of hardship and, sometimes, danger. If you were desperately concerned that you might really die of cold, then I am quite sure you would have allowed me to swim to shore and find a boat. There!" The comte sat back on his heels with a grunt of satisfaction as the brush caught, and a satisfying yellow and red flame sprang up.

"Now, you may sit at the fire," he went on, "or you may help me find more wood, an exercise which will serve to warm you."

Without waiting to see what she was going to do, he set about finding dead branches and breaking them and arranging them in a pile beside the fire.

Delphine's nerves were completely overset by the danger she had been in and by his outrageous callousness. She stood up, marched over to him, and boxed him on the ear as hard as she could.

He caught her wrist and looked down at her, his eyes glinting dangerously in the moonlight.

Then he said mildly, "You are not really much help in an emergency," and went on breaking wood.

Delphine stood with her hands clenched at her sides, feeling suddenly miserable and deflated. With her head averted from him, she began to pick up sticks and throw them on the fire. At last she said in a low voice, "I am sorry, Jules. I did not mean to strike you."

He gave her a bow. "Your apology is accepted. There is nothing more beneficial, however, than a good outburst of temper when one has escaped death and is wearing an evening gown and little else."

Delphine blushed and glanced down at herself. Her gown and pelisse were pasted to her body, leaving little of her figure to the imagination.

The blaze climbed higher. At last the comte sat down beside the fire. Delphine sat down beside him, stretching out her hands to the warmth.

"Perhaps someone will see the fire and come to investigate," he said, putting an arm around her.

Delphine made to shrug it off, but decided almost at the same moment that she had already behaved badly enough. If what he had said was true, that the highwaymen would have killed them if they could, then he had saved her life.

But underneath, a niggling, peevish, feminine voice was still complaining that it was all his fault, and if he had waited on her pleasure at Manchester Square as he was supposed to do, then she wouldn't have been on the Richmond road in the middle of the night in the first place.

He dropped his arm from her shoulder and shrugged out of his wet coat. He rolled it into a pillow. "Oh, my beautiful new clothes." He sighed. "How proud I was of them!"

"I shall buy you more," said Delphine quickly.

"Money does not solve every problem," he said gently. "There are some ruined and broken things it cannot mend."

He lay down and pillowed his head on his coat. "Join me," he said. "I am going to sleep."

"You can't just go to sleep at a time like this!" cried Delphine.

"I am so tired, I could sleep through an earthquake," he murmured sleepily. "If you insist on staying awake, remember to put more wood on the fire."

Delphine glared down at him. Any *gentleman*, she thought angrily, would be worried sick about her welfare. Did this wretched man think she was made of steel?

But he fell almost immediately into a quiet, soundless sleep. Delphine wrapped her arms around her legs and stared into the fire. And then, as the fire crackled and roared, she was suddenly transported back in time. She could feel the cold of a stone floor under her bare feet, hear the crackling, roaring whoosh as the château was set alight, hear the screaming, screaming, screaming, and under it all the cackles and yells of the mob.

The vision left as quickly as it had come. She started to shiver again. An owl hooted from the woods on the shore, and every plop of a rising fish seemed like the sound of a dipped oar as the highwaymen glided along the river, looking for their prey.

Delphine crept to where her husband lay sleeping so peacefully. She curled into his side and put her head on his chest. He stirred in his sleep and mumbled something and put both arms tightly around her.

Gradually, Delphine's shaking and shivering subsided. The fire blazed away merrily, and she was just thinking about disengaging herself and going to put on more wood when her eyes closed and she fell fast asleep.

A shrill voice, calling from the riverbank, woke both of them several hours later. Delphine stared wildly about. A gray dawn was spreading over the sky. Mist was rising from the river and curling around the boles of the trees. The fire was nearly out.

The comte cocked his head on one side and listened intently.

"Guvner!" came another faint cry.

"Charlie!" said the comte. "Thank God he's safe."

He ran over the island. Charlie was standing on the parapet of the bridge, his diminutive figure in its new livery appearing and disappearing in the writhing mist.

"Get a boat!" shouted the comte.

Charlie waved and disappeared.

The comte went back and found Delphine putting wood on the fire. Her gown had shrunk, and she was exhibiting a neat pair of ankles.

"Charlie will find a boat," said the comte. "Your ordeal will soon be over."

Delphine bent her head and searched in her reticule for a comb, suddenly shy of him.

She pulled the comb through her tangled locks, first removing the last remaining silk rose.

The mist turned yellow and gold as the sun came up.

The comte watched her as she combed her hair.

"Your hair ordinarily looks brown," he said reflectively, "but then one notices it has little gold lights in it. Fascinating!"

Delphine flushed and put the comb back in her reticule.

"We will soon be back in London," he went on in a kindly voice, "and then we can go on our separate ways."

Delphine did not know what to say. One part of her longed to run back to the old life at Marsham Manor; the other wanted to try to make the marriage work, if only in honor of her parents' memory, she told herself severely.

Then they heard the rhythmic sound of oars moving in rowlocks, and soon Charlie's figure in a small green boat could be seen rounding the island.

He beached the boat and jumped out on the little beach, grinning all over his face.

"Knew'd I'd find you hale and hearty," he crowed.

"Everyone seems to have more faith in my stamina than I have myself," said Delphine tartly.

"What happened?" asked the comte, ignoring her.

"Well, soon as you both landed in the drink," said Charlie, "them high pads runs frough the carridge and out the door you just quit.

"They're standing on the bridge with their pistols cocked, peering at the water, so the coachman whips up the horses and off we goes. Couldn't help you by staying, because that fool of a coachman has a pistol, but it's so old and rusty it's no good to anyone. We stops at the nearest roundhouse and raises the alarm, but by the time the men gets back, them high pads has gone. The coachman and grooms ups and says they ain't your servants but belongs of Monsoor Duclos, and *they* ups and offs. Everyone else tells me it's ten to one you're dead, and *they* ups and offs. But I knew you, guvner, so I decided to wait till morning. Which I did."

"Well, we'd best get ashore and find some sort of transport back to London," said the comte, grinning. He picked up his jacket and unrolled it, looking ruefully at the dirt and creases.

"Leave it," said Delphine. "It's ruined."

"I may be able to do something with it," he answered, tossing the coat into the boat.

Delphine watched him covertly as the tiger rowed them towards the shore.

The comte's gold curls were being ruffled by the morning breeze. His face showed no signs of strain whatsoever. The thin cambric of his shirt revealed the breadth of his chest. His eyes were blue and carefree. He did not seem to have a care in the world.

That was what rankled.

He didn't seem to care in the slightest about his new bride.

It was as if he had finally come to a decision in his mind that the marriage had never existed.

Delphine pictured him going back to his old life with hardly a thought for her.

She had a childish desire to catch his attention.

"I have most likely caught the ague," she remarked.

"No. You have a fine color which owes nothing to fever," he said. "In fact I would say the experience has improved your looks."

Delphine had an impulse to burst into tears.

There was a humiliating time to be gone through while Charlie returned the boat to its owner in Richmond, and she had to endure the stares of the early morning passersby.

Then at the livery stable the owner wanted a sizeable deposit for a horse and carriage, going so far as to say he had kept his trade solvent from being able to tell the villains from the right 'uns.

"You are *not* going to sleep *again*," protested Delphine sharply when they were finally seated in the carriage.

"But of course, my sweeting," he said amiably. "I am tired. I am always tired. Furthermore, since we are shortly about to part company, I do not see why you should wish for my conversation."

Delphine was prey to a series of conflicting emotions. Why could he not realize she had ambivalent feelings towards this marriage?

"You never told me about my parents," she said.

There was a silence, and, for a moment, she really thought he was asleep. But finally he said, "I did not see much of them. I remember you vaguely. You were a fat little thing, always falling over the furniture."

"Fat!" said Delphine, outraged. Somehow she had thought of herself as being a slim, waiflike child, all eyes.

"Yes, fat," he said sleepily. "And very rude. You were thoroughly spoilt. You expected me to play silly games with you any time I went on a visit. I did not want to, but my parents pointed out that you were a rich baby who would one day inherit the de Fleuris lands because there was no male heir, and so I had to play with you. But now I am heading rapidly for middle age and I do not have to play with you if I don't want to."

His eyes began to close again.

"Would you not like to see Marsham Manor?" asked Delphine in a voice that quavered slightly.

He reached forward and took her hand and kissed it gently. "Later," he said. "Not now." And with that he composed himself for sleep.

Delphine tried to decide what to do. But her head began to nod and soon she was fast asleep as well, not waking until they were clattering along Oxford Street.

After she had bathed and changed in the dingy flat in Manchester Square, she sat down at the dressing table to brush her hair and think things over. The comte had changed first, saying he had a call to make but promising to return within the hour.

Not for the first time did Delphine ponder over the mad impulse which had prompted her to marry a man she had never seen before. She decided at last that she must have been overset by the news of the manner of her parents' death. Then, any formal and lengthy arrangements would have involved Maria Bencastle. Also the call of the past was strong. She had been convinced that any man chosen for her by her parents must be perfect.

After all the work and worry of the estates, she knew now that she also had had a longing to be a child again, to have her decisions made for her.

Sir George had cosseted her and protected her too much. She realized that now. He should have let her meet her compatriots. He should have told her about her parents' death and let her listen to the other terrible stories of the Terror. Children who are protected too much from care and pain and responsibility are apt to remain children, and such was the case with Delphine. She had rushed blindly into the marriage simply because she wanted someone to take care of her as Sir George had done.

Instead, she was wed to Jules Saint-Pierre, who dragged her over rooftops and expected her to survive a plunge into the river without even a maidenly scream.

She realized now she had not really wanted frivolity and excitement. She had wanted an escape from responsibility.

If only he would rant and rave and insist that the marriage stand. If only he might lie a little and pretend to love her so that she might save face.

But she knew he would not command; neither would he beg or plead.

If she wanted to try to make the marriage work, then she would need to tell him so.

But did she want to continue with it? A vision of Jules juggling in the middle of Littlejohn Square flashed before her eyes. What on earth would people think of him? Did it matter what people thought of him? What did *she* think of him?

Delphine buried her aching head in her hands. Somehow it was better not to think. The very thought of him created such a jumble in her brain.

But surely she could change him. Surely she could turn him into the same sort of man that Sir George had been, quiet, unassuming, and protective.

A sound in the other room alerted her that her husband had returned.

Taking a deep breath, she rose and went to join him.

He was wearing a new coat of bottle green with a smart buff waistcoat, leather breeches, and new Hessian boots.

His linen was of the finest, and his golden hair was arranged artistically in the Windswept.

"You are looking very fine," said Delphine shyly.

"I am lucky. I bought these clothes from a friend with gambling debts who is of my size and could not afford to pay his tailor," he said cheerfully. "Madame de Manton paid me the money she owed me, and so I was not only able to buy this finery but to pay off my creditors."

"Indeed!" said Delphine acidly. "And just who, pray, is Madame de Manton?"

"A friend," he said simply. "The lady who took me to Mrs. Brandenbaugh's at Richmond. Her horses ran fleet at Newmarket for once."

"The very day after you are become wed," said Delphine, her eyes blazing, "you go to a party with some woman to whom I have not even been introduced!"

"I know a great number of ladies to whom you have not been introduced. Madame de Manton for one. She remembers your parents, and mine."

"Oh, an *old* woman," said Delphine, her face clearing.

"Ah, Delphine, you give me all the sorrows of marriage and none of the pleasures. Jealousy being one of them."

"Jealous! I! I have not one jealous bone in my whole body."

"Then what are we arguing about?"

"I am not arguing!"

"Then what *are* you doing?"

Delphine clenched her fists and glared at him. "I am simply trying to point out to you the error of your ways," she said in a voice which sounded horribly pompous even to her own ears. "Did you not stop to think that your behavior was irregular?"

"No," he said calmly, "in view of the fact I thought you had up and left me. In any case, I have paid my shot to that old witch, Mrs. Jenkins, and so I can return to my room. Charlie awaits me downstairs. I have not yet told him that he must once again face a future without horses, but no doubt he will survive."

"Your parents wished this marriage," said Delphine, twisting the folds of her muslin gown between her fingers.

"Of course they did, God bless 'em! I do not make a habit of joining myself in holy wedlock with just anyone who takes my fancy. But they did not plan this marriage because they thought we should suit. How could they, when you were little more than a baby at the time? They meant one large piece of land should ultimately be joined to another large piece of land. But sentimentality took me by the throat, I must admit. Well, what is done can be undone."

"I am going to Marsham Manor today," said Delphine desperately.

"I wish you Godspeed."

"You are not helping me *at all*. I hate you," said Delphine stormily.

"I could not possibly be more helpful," he replied, crossing to the glass and admiring the set of his cravat with infuriating aplomb. "You do not want me in your life. *Voilà!* I am removing myself."

"I did not say I did not want you," mumbled Delphine.

"I beg your pardon?"

"I said, 'I did not say I did not want you!'" shouted poor Delphine, quite scarlet with embarrassment.

"As what? Not as a lover."

"Sit down. I cannot possibly talk to you when you go on preening in the looking glass in that sickening way."

"Very well." He threw himself into a chair and clasped his long fingers around his knees and surveyed her amiably.

"I do not think the vows we made to each other

should be lightly put aside," said Delphine, sitting opposite him but not meeting his eyes. "Perhaps we should spend some more time together to see if this marriage might work. I . . . I have a great deal of responsibility since Sir George died."

"Which you wish me to assume? Have you not a steward or bailiff?"

"Yes, a Mr. Garnett. He is a good man."

"Then what is the problem? The responsibility has become his. As our English hosts point out, what is the point of keeping a dog and barking yourself?"

"It makes a difference," said Delphine severely, "when the land that you care for is not yours. No matter how good the steward, the master must be deeply concerned with the heart of the land, or the estates will not prosper."

"I would like to be able to make my own decisions," he said with unimpaired good humor. "I would like a good, long rest, and then we shall see. Are you prepared to have me on those terms?"

Delphine traced the faded pattern of the oriental carpet with the toe of her slipper—along the dragon's back, along the dragon's nose. . . .

"Yes," she said abruptly, all the while planning how she would change and mold him in the image of Sir George.

Chapter Six

No one at Marsham Manor welcomed the arrival of the new master. It seemed as if even the weather were in mourning. Since the comte's arrival, it had rained steadily, soaking, depressing, gray rain, a relentless downpour which chuckled in the lead gutters and spread pools on the lawns and made everything indoors damp to the touch.

With the exception of Maria Bencastle, no one had actually voiced any disapproval. But it was there, in the scowls of the servants, in the careful courtesy of her new steward, in the sidelong looks Delphine received in the marketplace.

Delphine would have culled some bitter enjoyment from the situation had her husband seemed in the slightest way aware of it. But true to his word, he slept and slept, arriving downstairs only for meals.

In order to bring him to some guilty awareness of his sloth, Delphine began to work harder than she had ever done before she had a steward. Mr. Garnett confided to his assistant that her ladyship was *making* work, but to the uninitiated of the county, it made Delphine look like a martyr. Feelings already ran high against foreigners in general and the French in particular, and now the whole weight of xenophobia was centered on the uncaring shoulders of the Comte Saint-Pierre.

The servants at Marsham Manor could barely conceal their dislike. And everywhere about the local countryside went Maria Bencastle, scandalizing and tattling about how Delphine had been tricked into marrying a penniless nobody. "Every one of the Frenchies," said Maria wisely, "says they're a prince or a count, but they were probably plain Mr. Jones back in their own country."

Jules Saint-Pierre hardly spoke to his wife on the rare occasions he saw her. When not downstairs eating, he was upstairs in his rooms with his head on a pillow and his eyes on a book.

He read and slept, and slept and read, and the rain continued to drum on the roof and run in greasy tears down the windows.

And then abruptly one morning, the rain stopped, the sun shone, and a family of blackbirds pulled fat worms out of the sodden grass in front of the drawing room windows.

Delphine slept late, not going downstairs until ten o'clock in the morning. The butler, Bradley, silently indicated a folded note lying next to her breakfast plate.

Delphine opened it, saw it was from her husband, folded it again, and proceeded to eat her breakfast, much to Bradley's disappointment. The butler lingered as long as he could, but when her ladyship showed no signs of reading the note, he took himself off to the kitchens.

As soon as the door had closed behind him, Delphine snatched up the note. "'Dear Heart,'" she read,

"'I am gone to see what the countryside looks like and hope to have the pleasure of your company at dinner, Jules.'"

"If he behaves in his usual manner," thought Delphine with not very commendable malice, "then he is going to find out just how unpopular the French are around here!"

Maria Bencastle came striding in, dressed as usual in black from head to foot. Delphine crumpled the note.

"Where is your . . . er . . . *husband*?" demanded Mrs. Bencastle, eyeing the crumpled paper.

"He has gone out to see the countryside," said Delphine.

"Then he is in for a great shock," said Maria Bencastle with satisfaction. "I hear that folks hereabouts think he's a Bonapartist spy."

"What?" Delphine stared at Mrs. Bencastle in alarm, and then her eyes narrowed. "I wonder, Maria," she said, "I just wonder who on earth gave them that impression."

Mrs. Bencastle turned a dull red. "Well, stands to reason," she blustered. "What with Boney and all his troops marching towards Belgium, feelings are running high, and no one wanted the comte to come here anyway."

Only a brief moment before, Delphine had been relishing the idea of her husband's possible mortification. Now she was frightened and worried. In her mind's eye, she could see the angry mob stoning Jules in the Littlejohn market square.

"I had better ride out and look for him," she said. "Did he take his tiger?"

"If you mean that cheeky jackanapes . . . no. Master Charlie is lounging in front of the kitchen fire."

Delphine became more and more worried. She rushed upstairs to change into her riding dress. For all her worry, she did not don her old joseph but a green and gold riding habit. Somehow, she felt sure she would find Jules in Littlejohn. He seemed such a creature of the streets and buildings. Impossible to imagine him roaming the countryside.

Jules Saint-Pierre was, in fact, riding into Littlejohn. But he had spent over two hours riding along pleasant country lanes, admiring the view and listening to bird-song. He had many opportunities to reflect on the amazing surliness of the English peasant.

All his cheerful "Good days" were met with sullen silence and glowering looks. He had heard that the English agricultural laborer was more independent than his old French counterpart. He had not expected ser-vility. He had, however, expected a modicum of re-spect towards the new lord of the manor.

Perhaps he was not suited for the country after all, he thought as he rode into town. Perhaps he would meet with more civility in Littlejohn.

He swung down from his horse in the market square. The animosity towards him was almost tangible. There was a great crowd gathered for some event. Then he began to make out mutterings of "French spy," low at first but growing in volume.

Just as he was debating whether to beat an igno-minious retreat before he was stoned or torn to pieces, there came a welcome diversion, and all eyes turned away from him to the church steeple. The comte, who was a good head and shoulders above the crowd, watched with interest.

A stout rope had been stretched from the bell tower down to a ring and bolt in the center of the square. From the talk about him, he was able to gather what was about to happen.

The "Flying Man" had been a great event in the last century and still lingered on in the second decade of the nineteenth. It involved "flying" or sliding at great speed down a taut rope from as great a height as possible. It had largely gone out of favor because of the great number of deaths. Only too often had the performer ended up dashing himself to his death on the cobbles.

The comte craned his neck. The steeple seemed to swing against the great white clouds, which were flying across the windy, blue sky.

A small figure, foreshortened by the distance, appeared at the window of the bell tower. A great cheer went up from the crowd.

Then there was a breathless silence. All eyes were riveted on the figure of the performer.

And then he began to descend...very slowly, very cautiously, hand over hand.

The crowd watched in increasing disappointment until he finally reached the ground. And then a great jeer of contempt broke from every throat.

Forgetting his rank and his new position in society, the comte remarked as one street performer to another, "Not a very good show."

"Oh, it ain't, eh?" said a burly man. "Think you can do better than an Englishman, you French *spy!*"

"Yes, come along, let's see if monsoor can do better," screeched an elderly harridan.

The mood of the crowd grew ugly. Out of the corner of his eye, Jules Saint-Pierre saw a man bend and prise loose a cobble.

"If I prove I can do better," he said in his light, easy voice, which carried well across the crowd, "then you will tell me how this slander of my being a spy came about. Now, make way for the expert," he said with a sunny grin.

Muttering and uneasy and nonplussed, the crowd fell back.

"He'll never do it," shouted one. "He's going to escape."

"Not I!" the comte shouted back over his shoulder

as he strode in the direction of the church.

"He be ever so handsome," said a country girl, sighing. "He don't look like a Frenchie at all."

Several men had shouldered their way into the church after the comte. They did not think for a minute he meant to go through with it. Only look at his clothes! That alone showed the man to be dishonest. Even Mr. Bryce-Connell had never looked so fine.

The comte was wearing the clothes he had bought from his gambling friend. His bottle-green morning coat was stretched across his shoulders without a wrinkle, his new Hessian boots were polished to perfection, his cravat was a sculptured miracle.

But the comte went over to the stairs to the belfry and began to climb.

Outside the crowd was frantically discussing how the rumors about the new lord of Marsham Manor had started.

No one could quite think of where they had heard that the Comte Saint-Pierre was a spy, except that "someone had said it."

It was Mr. Partington who suddenly shouted shrilly, "It was Mrs. Bencastle who told *me*." There was a silence while everyone turned and looked at the owner of the haberdashery store. "Well, it *was*," continued Mr. Partington, delighted to be the center of attention. "She used to tell me that Lady Charteris had entrapped poor Sir George as well, but I never did pay heed to that, either. Mrs. Bencastle never has a good word for anyone. She said I sold shoddy goods...."

"So you do," shouted Mr. Cutler, the red-faced butcher.

"She said you sold horses meat and called it beef," shrieked Mr. Partington. "Yes. Yes. And...and she said Widow Giles was no widow and had never been married. And...and...she said vicar was too friendly with his housekeeper and..."

"Enough," growled a farmer. "We all know Mrs. Bencastle's an evil gossip."

"But *you* don't, do you?" said Mr. Partington wildly. "You believed her about the comte, didn't you? And you were nigh to killing him, weren't you? And now he'll probably die anyway, and it'll all be your fault!" And with that, the much overwrought haberdasher burst into noisy tears.

What had been a wild and murderous mob such a short time before was now a collection of shamefaced, worried country people.

"There he is!" cried a boy, and with a terrible sort of dread, leaning together, bunching together, as if to ease their guilt by sharing it; people huddled close, shoulder to shoulder, gazing anxiously up at the church.

"Run and tell them it's all a mistake," the farmer who had spoken before said to a small boy. "Run up there and stop him before it's too late."

"It *is* too late!" said a hollow voice behind him.

Up at the belfry tower, the comte edged to the very edge of the belfry window.

"Don't!" screamed a woman.

And then they all held their breath.

Suddenly, the comte seemed to fall forward onto the rope and then he started to hurtle towards them, face down on the rope, his hands outspread.

His booted legs were firmly wrapped around the rope at the back, but to the watching crowd it appeared that he was flying down towards them at a tremendous rate, any second to be dashed against the cobbles.

There rose a great wail of despair when he showed no signs of being able to stop. People tried to wrench their eyes away but found them glued to the flying figure, hurtling down from above.

It seemed he was but a few inches from certain death when he suddenly and magically slowed and, with a tremendous somersault, he landed on his feet in front of them as lightly as a cat, the sun shining on his golden curls, and his merry blue eyes raking over the crowd.

They cheered and cheered and fought with each other for the honor of shaking his hand.

"I want to make a speech!" called the comte at last.

A stool was produced, and the comte jumped up on it and faced the crowd.

"Now," he said, "who has been calling me a spy? I have not been back to France since my parents were killed in the Terror. I am a Royalist. Why should I work for Napoleon Bonaparte?"

"It was Mrs. Bencastle," shouted Mr. Partington. "She told us. She said all sorts of things. *I* didn't listen to her. Not I."

"I wondered how you all recognized me enough to hate me," said the comte mildly. "Mrs. Bencastle must have described my appearance also."

There were vigorous nods.

"Well, I do not want my wife distressed by all this," the comte went on. He leaned forward and addressed a fascinated urchin at the edge of the crowd. "Do you know what happens to people who gossip?" he asked.

The boy shook his head dumbly.

The comte leaned further forward. "I'll tell you. They end up with heads full of cotton." And in front of the amazed crowd he appeared to pull a long length of cambric handkerchief from the child's ear.

More children pushed to the front. "Oh, milord," squeaked a tiny, grubby girl. "Do some more."

The comte smiled at the children. He felt the sun on his back, felt the warmth towards him emanating from the now adoring crowd, saw the wide eyes of the little children, and forgot that he was now an English aristocrat with lands and people under him. Once again, he was Monsoor Jules of the street fairs. A mocking, teasing smile curled his lips. His hand went to the pocket in the pleats of his coat; out came six silver balls, which he proceeded to juggle while the crowd cheered and roared.

And that was how Delphine found her husband.

She had ridden desperately to Littlejohn, her worry rising by the minute. She was frantic with anxiety by the time she gained the town square and heard the roar of the crowd.

She fully expected to see Jules Saint-Pierre swinging from a lamppost.

But there he was, debonair and laughing, juggling balls in front of a cheering crowd.

She swung down from her horse and pushed her way through to the front of the crowd, her face flaming with anger.

A nightmare had come true. Instead of behaving with dignity, like Sir George, the comte was carrying on as if he had never left the poverty of the street fairs of London.

Before she reached him, Delphine saw Harriet Bryce-Connell and her brother standing up in their open carriage on the far side of the square. Harriet was laughing and applauding, and even her brother looked amused.

Delphine felt her humiliation was complete. Too angry to realize she would make matters more disgraceful by creating a scene, she elbowed and pushed her way until she was standing under him.

"Stop it this minute!" she snapped.

The comte deftly caught the balls and returned them to his pocket.

"The show is over, my children," he said with a kind smile.

"You fool!" hissed Delphine. "Must you always disgrace me? Must you behave like a ragamuffin?"

"So many questions," he murmured, jumping lightly down.

He started to walk with her through the crowd. People parted at their approach. The women dropped low curtsies to Delphine, and the men bowed low.

"Where is your horse, sirrah?" demanded Delphine.

"By some fortuitous chance, my sweeting," he said, "my horse is tethered next to yours."

"Then mount and ride. I am taking you home. You must be taught how to behave yourself!"

By this time, Delphine was holding his arm in a firm clasp.

He stopped and took her hand from his arm and bent his head and kissed it.

"But I am not ready to go home yet." He smiled. "I am extremely thirsty and I see a hostelry over there."

"Have you no shame?" yelled Delphine, stamping her foot.

"I think I would certainly be ashamed if I were found behaving like a fishwife, ranting and raving in public," he said. "But since that is not the case, I feel remarkably free from guilt. Do you care to share a glass of wine with me?"

"Be damned to you," hissed Delphine, scarlet with embarrassment and now all too aware of the multitude of listening ears.

She turned on her heel and marched away.

The comte proceeded at a leisurely pace towards the Wheatsheaf. He espied the thin, nervous figure of the haberdasher, Mr. Partington, who was bowing so low his nose nearly touched the cobbles.

The comte stopped and raised his quizzing glass. "Ah, the gentleman who so kindly identified the name of the gossip," he said.

"Mr. William Partington, haberdasher, at your service, milord," said Mr. Partington as best as he could, for he was still doubled over in a deep bow.

"Then perhaps, Mr. Partington, you would care to join me in a bottle of wine?" said the comte. Mr. Partington straightened up, his mouth hanging open in amazement. The comte smiled at him gently and tucked Mr. Partington's arm into his own and proceeded on his way.

Mr. Partington held his head high, tears of pride starting out of his eyes. Mrs. Partington was not present on this momentous occasion, but she was to hear about "The Day I Took Wine with the Comte Saint-Pierre" for the rest of her days, so it was probably just as well that the poor woman was to be spared this agony for a little longer.

Delphine walked up and down in front of Marsham Manor, the long skirt of her riding dress swishing across the grass. She was furious with Jules and furious with herself, although she felt she had somehow been tricked into making a disgraceful public scene. What on earth had happened to her? She, who had never been known to raise her voice.

How *could* he behave so?

After some time, she became aware of a figure flitting silently through the trees at the edge of the lawn, a figure that seemed to be keeping pace with her.

She stopped abruptly and called out, "Who are you? Who's there?"

"It's me, missus." The tiger, Charlie, poked his head around a tree trunk and surveyed her.

"Come here!" commanded Delphine.

The tiger sidled towards her across the grass with an ingratiating smile on his face.

"Why are you watching me?" demanded Delphine. "And in future, address me as 'my lady' when you speak to me."

"Yes, missus," said the reprehensible Charlie, giving her a servile smirk, infuriating in its hypocrisy.

"Well, I am waiting," said Delphine. "Why were you watching me?"

"I was waiting for you to calm down, like," said the tiger, "so's I could tell you what really 'appened."

"Explain yourself!"

"Well, I got it from the knife boy what was down in the town..." Leaning nonchalantly against the sundial, Charlie proceeded to give a long and rambling account of the comte's marvelous flying dive, how he had to do it to stop the crowd from stoning him, and how it had been discovered that Mrs. Bencastle had been going about saying the comte was a Bonapartist spy.

"Did he *have* to go through with all these vulgar acrobatics?" demanded Delphine haughtily. "Would it not have been wiser to take flight?"

"Wot good would that ha' done," said Charlie scornfully. "They would've followed him to the manor, that they would, and we would ha' had another o' them French revulsions."

"Thank you for your explanation," said Delphine frostily. "Where is Mrs. Bencastle to be found?"

"In the drawing room, miss...my lady."

Delphine marched across the wet grass and into the drawing room by way of the french windows.

She stood glaring across the room at the squat, black-clothed figure of Maria Bencastle.

Mrs. Bencastle looked up and quailed before the look of fury on Delphine's face.

Delphine began to speak in slow and measured tones. She took Maria Bencastle's character apart, shred by shred; she berated her for a malicious gossip who had nearly caused the death of the comte, and she did not pause for breath for quite half an hour.

Maria Bencastle began to cry. Gasping and babbling, she said she had only been trying to drive the comte away, because he was so obviously making Delphine unhappy. And he was so lazy! Never had anyone seen a man sleep so much!

It had been maddening, sobbed Maria wretchedly, to see Delphine working so hard while her husband slept and slept. Maddening to see her poor angel, Delphine, become dowdy and wasted.

"Dowdy!" exclaimed Delphine, her hands going to her face.

"So ill-looking," corrected Maria hastily.

She, Maria Bencastle, had done wrong; that she freely admitted. But it had been for the best motives, the very best.

On and on she went, begging and pleading, so unlike her usual grumpy self that Delphine was at last abashed. She insisted, however, that Mrs. Bencastle should make a full apology to the comte and promise to ride about the countryside and repair as much of the damage that she had already done as she could.

And Mrs. Bencastle, who was in fact terrified at the idea of having to live alone, promised *anything* so long as she could stay at Marsham Manor.

Delphine left her and decided to spend the rest of the day in the estates' office, going over the books. Mr. Garnett and his assistant, Tom Bowyer, were out on one of the farms, so she knew she would be alone.

But she found it increasingly hard to concentrate on the columns of figures as the day began to darken outside, as the evening shadows lengthened, and there was still no sign of her husband coming home.

She sent word to the kitchens that dinner was to be put back until eight in the evening, an impossibly late hour even by London standards. Surely he would be home by then.

At last, by seven, she became aware she was still in her riding dress and went abovestairs to change into an evening gown. It was of burgundy-colored silk, cut low on the bosom, with worked embroidery of dull gold, and it had a short train at the back.

She fastened a collar of garnets around her neck and brushed and twisted her hair into an elaborate confection on top of her head. She had to admit the dark wine color became her. Her golden skin glowed against the richness of the material, and, with great daring, she slightly rouged her lips.

She was just putting another pin into her hair to

make sure the elaborate style was more secure when she heard her husband arriving home.

She ran to the window and looked out.

He swung down from his horse and stood talking to Charlie for a few moments. Then Charlie led his horse away in the direction of the stables, and the comte entered the house.

She could hear him mounting the stairs and then his steps retreating along the passageway in the direction of his rooms.

Delphine found that her hands were shaking slightly, and frowned severely at her reflection in the looking glass. She owed her husband an apology. But at the same time, he must be made to realize that conduct more befitting to his new station in life was expected of him.

She went slowly down to the drawing room.

After she had been waiting five minutes, he walked in lazily, putting up one long hand to stifle a yawn.

His eyes widened slightly at her appearance. "You look extremely beautiful." He smiled. "Such a transformation! One would never take you for the red-faced harridan that screamed at me so awfully in the middle of the town square."

Delphine bit back an angry retort and said instead in measured tones, "Pray take my arm, sir, and escort me in to dinner. It has been waiting this age."

"Do not trouble on my account," he said amiably as they walked across the hall. "I dined at the Wheatsheaf. Cannot stomach the food here. It doesn't matter how new it is or how long it's been waiting. It always tastes as if it had been cooked last week in an overhot oven."

"I am sorry our food does not suit your pampered palate," said Delphine, entering the dining room ahead of him and sitting in a high-backed chair at the end of the dining table. He sat at the other end and stifled another yawn.

"It is obvious," Delphine went on, "that we cannot hope to cope with the gastronomic delights of Soho."

"Oh, I don't see why not. I cook very well myself," he said. "I shall join you in some wine, nonetheless, and I admire your stamina in eating the dreadful stuff."

"I think you have had enough wine already," said Delphine, noticing the glitter in his blue eyes.

"Never enough," he said lazily, filling his glass.

Bradley and two footmen came in with the dishes.

"Is Mrs. Bencastle not favoring us with her charming presence this evening?" asked the comte. Bradley stiffened and the footmen stood with faces like wood. All had heard of Mrs. Bencastle's malice and the comte's exploits in Littlejohn.

"No, I believe she had a tray in her room," said Delphine. "His lordship is not eating, Bradley. You need not trouble to serve him."

Delphine forced herself to talk of general things until the servants had retired.

Finally, she looked straight at her husband and said, "Jules, I owe you an apology."

"My heart?"

"Yes, I am sorry I berated you in public. I did not have the true facts of the case and thought you were entertaining the crowd because . . . because you did not know how to behave like a gentleman."

"It is a difficult apology to accept," he said.

"I mean," Delphine went on desperately, "not that you do not know how to behave like a gentleman, it is just that, in the past, you were forced to earn your own living, and I thought you had forgotten that such things were not necessary anymore."

"By George!" he said. "I never thought of that. Best audience I ever had. Should have had Charlie there to take 'round the hat."

"Jules!"

"Apology accepted," he said, filling his glass again. "I am monstrous tired."

"A great deal of wine makes anyone tired!" Delphine rose to her feet. "And now, if you will excuse me, my lord, I must retire."

He stood up, nodding to her vaguely, and ambled down the length of the room to where she was standing.

He suddenly clipped her around the waist and drew her close against him. "Jules," whispered Delphine, "you must not..."

His mouth came down on her own, his lips moving slowly and sensually against hers. Her heart was beating wildly, and her whole body was trembling and shaking, buffeted by terrible physical wrenchings and longings.

"I *am* sorry," he said, suddenly freeing her and standing back. "The fact is, I am a trifle foxed. It will not happen again. Fie! What you must think of me. Fie, for *shame!*"

"Very well, Jules," said Delphine jerkily. "Simply let me retire."

"By all means, my heart."

He walked with her across the hall and up the stairs. "There is no need to come with me as far as my room..." Delphine began, when a door in the passageway opened and Maria Bencastle appeared. She was wearing a black nightdress and a black nightcap perched on top of a forest of curl papers. Delphine was used to Mrs. Bencastle's eccentricity in dress—after all the woman had been wearing mourning for years—but the effect on the comte was startling.

He let out a wild scream and backed down the passageway. "Oh, *God*," he screamed, putting his hands in front of his face like Kean playing Macbeth in the banquet scene. "What hellish spirit is this! What dreadful apparition! Angels and ministers of grace defend us!"

"It is Mrs. Bencastle," said Delphine, wondering whether to laugh or cry. "Jules, *please*..."

"No! No!" he wailed. "That horror is nothing human. That great ugly black mound of putrefaction. Those glaring eyes. Oh, horrors!"

"Oh, *fiddle!*" snapped Maria Bencastle, red with fury. She went back into her room and slammed the door.

"Goodness," said the comte, passing a shaking hand across his brow. "Thank heavens that terrible apparition has gone. I have never been so frightened in my life."

"You have never been so infuriating in all your life," said Delphine. "I did not know you had added high melodrama to your other talents."

"Ah, my sweeting," said the comte mournfully. "When will you *ever* take me seriously?"

"When will you *ever* take yourself seriously?" rejoined Delphine.

But he only gave her a slight wave of his hand, turned the corner of the passageway, and was gone.

"I shall *never* get him to behave," thought Delphine. "*Never!*"

Chapter Seven

❖

*Delphine did not see her husband at the break-*fast table the next morning and assumed he had gone back to his lethargic ways. It was with some surprise that she was to learn from Charlie that he had been up at dawn and gone off with Mr. Garnett, the steward.

Delphine was annoyed. If Jules wished to take an interest in the estates, then he should have consulted her first.

There was a noisy, blustery, restless wind blowing outside. The trees tossed their boughs up to the turbulent sky. The head gardener, MacGregor, was weeding a flowerbed; the maids and footmen were going about their chores. All at once, there seemed to be nothing to do.

After another hour of idleness, Delphine welcomed the visit of Farmer Yardley and Farmer Stone. Even their crazy way of fighting, with her as referee, was better than doing nothing at all.

She had Bradley put both men in the estates' office and was making her way there when she met the large figure of her husband entering the hall.

"Good morning, Jules," she said demurely. "I will be with you presently. I have some business to attend to."

"Which is?"

"Which is dealing with two of my tenant farmers who refuse to speak to each other and ask me to relay their insults, since they will not talk to each other directly."

"And how long has this been going on?" asked the comte curiously.

"Oh, forever." Delphine shrugged. "It does not take very much of my time."

"I will see to them," said the comte.

"No," Delphine said, laughing, "you cannot possibly handle..."

"If I am to help you," he said with unexpected firmness, "then you must trust me."

"Very well." Delphine gave in with bad grace. "But I am coming with you."

Farmer Yardley and Farmer Stone rose to their feet at the couple's entrance, looking taken aback at the sight of the comte.

Jules Saint-Pierre was wearing a venerable riding coat, worn moleskin breeches, and high top boots. He had exchanged his usual snowy cravat in favor of a simple linen kerchief tied about his throat. His shirt was of coarse, unbleached linen.

Delphine realized he owned very few clothes indeed.

"Now," said the comte pleasantly, sitting down behind the large cluttered desk which dominated the room and indicating that the two farmers should sit in chairs facing him. Delphine sat over by the window.

Farmer Yardley placed his round hat on his knees and cleared his throat. "It's like this, my lord. I want you to tell this scoundrel here that cow of his was not *straying* on my land but let in there deliberate-like so as to annoy me."

"Very well," said the comte. He turned to Farmer Stone. "You are a scoundrel, sir," he said suddenly and venomously, "and you put that cow on my land simply to enrage me!"

Farmer Stone turned dark red. "Now look here, my lord," he replied, "you just tell this long-nosed good-for-nothing that he sees ill in everyone's innocent actions because that's the way he thinks himself."

The comte rounded on Farmer Yardley. "See here, you long-nosed, useless milksop," he said viciously, "how dare you judge my actions according to those of your own spite-filled, little mind."

It was Farmer Yardley's turn to color beet red.

"You tell him, my lord," he mumbled, "that if he apologizes, we won't say no more about the matter."

"Apologize, you dim-witted fool!" grated the comte.

"I ain't got nothing to apologize for," bleated Farmer Stone nervously.

"I've got nothing to apologize for, you brainless scum," roared the comte.

The two farmers sat and blinked at him like owls. Then there came a slow rumbling sound from deep inside Farmer Yardley. Delphine watched him nervously. The rumbling grew louder and suddenly exploded into a full-scale shout of laughter.

A slow smile dawned on Farmer Stone's face and then he began to laugh as well, until the two huge farmers were in danger of breaking the fragile chairs they sat on, they were shaking so much with laughter.

At last Farmer Yardley took out a large belcher handkerchief and mopped his streaming eyes and turned to Farmer Stone.

"Faith, Jimmy," he said, addressing his rival by his Christian name for the first time in history, "his lordship do make me feel like the gurtest fool."

"Me, too," said Farmer Stone with an unmanly giggle. "'Stead of wasting his lordship's time, let's go down to the Wheatsheaf and talk this over like sensible men. A bowl of rum punch, and I shall be host."

"Gladly." Both farmers rose to their feet. Farmer Yardley gave the comte and then Delphine an awkward bow. He glanced shyly at the comte and then burst out with, "I saw you yesterday, my lord. The way you flew down from that church steeple, well, I've never seen anything like it in all my born days."

"'Twas wonderful," chimed in Farmer Stone. "My heart was in my mouth."

"Spare my blushes." The comte laughed. "Mr. Yardley, tell my wife I think she is beautiful."

Farmer Yardley and Farmer Stone began to laugh again. "Now, now, my lord," said Farmer Yardley, waving an admonishing finger, "don't go making game of us agin."

Still laughing, the two farmers left arm in arm.

"Well, well," said the comte cheerfully, "that was all very simple."

"It will not last," said Delphine, who was angry at the ease with which he appeared to have resolved the situation.

"Oh, I think so," he replied. "They would feel utterly ridiculous doing the same thing again. Now, as to the matter of food in this residence. I feel it could be improved."

"Really?" said Delphine with a lift of the eyebrows. "We have been content with good English fare here."

"I have nothing against 'good English fare,'" rejoined her husband amiably, "provided it is properly cooked."

"We prefer to keep things as they were when Sir George was alive."

There was a moment's silence. "What a rude thing to say," said the comte thoughtfully.

Delphine flushed with embarrassment. "I meant that

we are set in our ways. The servants are old and are still devoted to Sir George's memory."

"It is the first time I have heard of the *cuisine* going into mourning." The comte's long, restless fingers began to play with a quill pen.

"There are English traditions I feel it would be undiplomatic to change," explained Delphine. "Some of the customs here have not changed much since Tudor times. Certain dishes belong to certain days. We have veal and a gammon of bacon and a tansy pudding on Easter day; a roast goose at Michaelmas; red herrings and salt fish with leeks, parsnips and pease pudding at Lent; at Martinmas, salt beef; at Midsummer, roast beef with butter and beans; at All Saints, pork and souse."

"It all sounds appetizing," commented the comte plaintively. "It's the production of which I complain."

The door opened as the butler entered. "Lady Gladstone," he announced.

Delphine looked flustered. "I have put her in the drawing room, my lord, my lady," said Bradley. "I assume a bottle of the *best* wine should be served?"

"Yes...oh, yes certainly, Bradley," said Delphine.

When the butler withdrew, the comte looked at her curiously. "You are all of a dither," he said. "What is so wonderful about this Lady Gladstone paying a social call?"

"She has never done so before. You see, she is a great figure in the county, almost as important as the Duke of Bedford. She disapproved of Sir George marrying me, and so she has never called before."

"She can't eat us," he said soothingly. "What woman could appear a dragon after meeting the redoubtable Mrs. Bencastle?"

"As to Mrs. Bencastle," said Delphine severely, "you behaved atrociously last night...screaming at the sight of her and calling her an apparition."

"Indeed, I must have been well to go." He smiled. "Can't remember a thing."

Lady Gladstone was examining the maker's mark on the bottom of a figurine as they entered the drawing room. She was an attractive-looking elderly woman with a good complexion and a mass of snow white hair. Her friendly, genial appearance belied her character, which was carping, domineering, and acidulous.

She was wearing a gray cambric gown over which she wore a gray levantine pelisse. On her white hair, she sported a Park carriage bonnet of white crêpe over white satin lined with a fluting of broad blond. The crown was finished with light gauze puffing; on the left side was a bunch of Provence roses, surmounted by a marabout plume of feathers.

Her pale eyes held the twinkling humorous look often adopted by people who have very little sense of humor.

"I am at last come to see you," she said with great condescension and not troubling to rise. Then she sat back a little in her chair and smiled benignly on both Delphine and the comte.

"Why?" The comte watched her with the bright, inquisitive look of a robin surveying a juicy worm.

"Why not?" parried Lady Gladstone gaily. "It is time I called to pay my respects."

"Oh, yes," said the comte. "I quite agree. But why *now* when you have not troubled before?"

"Well, really," bridled Lady Gladstone. "I would have thought my very presence was enough in itself."

"I do not agree," said the comte patiently.

"Jules!" muttered Delphine in an anguished voice, but he affected not to hear.

A series of conflicting expressions battled their way across Lady Gladstone's face. She had expected the newly married couple to be overwhelmed by the honor of her visit. Everyone was talking about the comte's exploits and bravery in the market square. She had always prided herself on being a leader of fashion, and if the comte were to be fashionable, she did not want to be left out.

And so she rushed on. "I am come to invite you both to my little *musicale*. To be held on Friday."

"This is Wednesday," the comte pointed out. "Do you normally hold such impromptu affairs?"

"Oh, yes," lied Lady Gladstone, who had planned this evening for some months and had had, until today, no intention of inviting the Comte Saint-Pierre or his wife.

Delphine eyed her husband nervously. She opened her mouth to accept, but the comte forestalled her and said quickly, "Unfortunately, we have a previous engagement for Friday. We are invited to Woburn."

"The duke!" exclaimed Lady Gladstone. "But *I* was not invited."

"It is only a small party for a very few friends," said the comte smoothly.

Delphine knew her husband was lying, but good manners stopped her from pointing out this fact in front of Lady Gladstone.

Lady Gladstone had not felt so flustered or put out for quite some time.

Instead of having all the joys of patronizing the Saint-Pierres, it seemed as if they were patronizing her. The comte was looking at her with a polite sort of social pity.

"No doubt the dear duke was aware of my little evening and knew I should not be free to attend," said Lady Gladstone, trying to keep the note of agony out of her voice.

"No doubt," said the comte with patently false politeness.

"Mr. and Miss Bryce-Connell," announced Bradley smugly. Minute by minute, the comte was becoming more of a hero in the Marsham Manor household. All the servants knew that it was thanks to his exploits in the marketplace that the county had started to call.

Harriet fluttered forward. "My dear Comtesse Saint-Pierre," she cooed. "*And* my dear comte. Such *fun* watching you yesterday. So brave!"

"'Pon rep, *yes!*" Geoffrey Bryce-Connell giggled, mincing across the room. "Wonderfulest thing I ever did see."

The couple then affected to notice Lady Gladstone for the first time.

Harriet shrewdly guessed Lady Gladstone had come to invite the Saint-Pierres to her *musicale*. She also guessed that Lady Gladstone had not told them the affair had been planned some time ago.

"We are looking forward to visiting you on Friday, Lady Gladstone," said Harriet. "Geoffrey thought I might have forgotten because you sent us your invitation such *ages* ago, but I said, 'My dear brother, how could I possibly forget an invitation from Lady Gladstone?'"

"How very odd," commented the comte lazily. "Lady Gladstone was just telling us it was an impromptu affair."

There was an awkward silence. "In any case, you cannot come because you are going to Woburn," said Lady Gladstone. "Tell me, Miss Bryce-Connell, what think you of..."

"Woburn!" Harriet interrupted, glancing sideways at her brother. "We cannot possibly compete with *that*. Geoffrey was just saying to Sir Giles Mancroft today that things at Marsham Manor have obviously changed—poor Sir George never went anywhere, you know—and that the Comte and Comtesse Saint-Pierre should be invited to the hunt ball next Wednesday.

"Sir Giles, *of course*, pointed out that invitations at the last minute are *so* rude, but I said, 'Never fear, Sir Giles, I am sure the Saint-Pierres will understand, and

Geoffrey and I will issue the invitation on your behalf.' Now, *do* say you will come."

"We should be delighted," said the comte blandly, ignoring a fulminating look from his wife.

Lady Gladstone was pink with embarrassment.

At that moment, the door opened, and Maria Bencastle lumbered in. She had had a dreadful time. She had gone to Littlejohn to shop at the haberdashery, and Mr. Partington had affected not to see her, so she had been unable to get any service. People had pointedly turned their backs on her in the street, and several children had cat-called after her, shouting, "Meddlesome, gossipy crow."

And now this! The comte sitting at his ease, entertaining the Bryce-Connells and Lady Gladstone.

Harriet's beautiful eyes filled with malice as they rested on Mrs. Bencastle. "I have just been inviting the Comte and Comtesse Saint-Pierre to the hunt ball on behalf of Sir Giles," she said. "They have graciously accepted."

"Oh, very well," said Maria ungraciously. "*I* am still in mourning. But I suppose it will be all right if I do not dance."

"Oh, but *you* are not invited, Maria," cooed Harriet. "After all those awful things you said about the comte being a spy, well, everyone always knew you had a wretched tongue, but they do feel you went a tiny bit too far this time."

"I do not gossip," poor Maria blustered. "It's all lies."

"Oh, but you do," said Lady Gladstone, delighted to turn attention away from herself. "You told us *all* that Sir George had made a dreadful mistake marrying a French nobody."

"And you did not encourage her one bit, either," put in the comte maliciously.

Lady Gladstone began to look flustered again. "My heavens! How time passes!" she exclaimed, getting abruptly to her feet. "Pray escort me to my carriage, my lord."

The comte walked out with her. "If having calls made on one," said Delphine to Harriet, "means having to endure a display of spite in one's own home, then I would rather be a recluse."

"But you should be used to that," exclaimed Harriet, raising her eyebrows. "I thought living with Maria would have inured you to it. Of course, we are all at fault and we did encourage Maria. She is so divinely malicious."

"I will not stay here another moment listening to this," said Maria Bencastle. "I thought you were my friend, Miss Bryce-Connell. Yes, I know you told me to call you 'Harriet' but that was when you were *pretending* to be my friend."

"For someone who says she is not going to stay another moment," said Harriet sweetly, "you are taking an unconscionable time in leaving."

"Wait!" said Delphine. "There is no need for you to leave, Maria. Mr. and Miss Bryce-Connell are going."

"Are we?" said Geoffrey Bryce-Connell, looking surprised.

Harriet opened her mouth to say something, caught the sparkling and militant look in Delphine's eyes, and stood up hurriedly.

"Come along, Geoffrey," she said, sailing towards the door. "We can say good-bye to the comte outside. Good-bye, Comtesse. Tell your fascinating husband that he must save at least one waltz for me."

When the door closed behind the Bryce-Connells, Delphine turned to Maria Bencastle, who was beginning to sob miserably.

"I think, Maria," she said gently, "that we will forget all the yesterdays and start from now. As far as I am concerned, you never said anything. That way we can be comfortable again."

But Maria Bencastle looked at her dumbly and then abruptly left the room.

"I hope that is the last call," thought Delphine. "I really do not think I can bear any more."

But during the day, carriages kept arriving in front of Marsham Manor, and the excited servants ran to and fro, carrying trays of tea and wine and cakes.

Maria Bencastle did not appear again. While carriages came and went, she sat in her room and nursed her injured pride. She was not a bad woman, only a very lonely, rather stupid woman with too much time on her hands who had always tried to rise in importance by criticizing other people.

She did not want Delphine's tolerance or forgiveness. Maria Bencastle wanted to be proved *right*. She desperately wanted the Comte Saint-Pierre to turn out to be a Bonapartist spy after all and so restore her standing in the community and in her own eyes.

She had meant to apologize to the comte. Now she found she could not. She blamed him for her day of humiliation, for it was inconceivable that she should blame herself.

Delphine did not have an opportunity to talk to her husband until dinner was served. She waited impatiently until the servants had withdrawn, took a deep breath, and started to berate her husband.

How *dare* he accept invitations without consulting her first? How dare he lie about them going to Woburn when she doubted that the Duke of Bedford even knew of their existence!

The comte surveyed her lazily, occasionally stifling a yawn, until at long last she had finished.

Then he picked up a bell beside his plate and rang it. Bradley entered so promptly it was almost as if he had been listening at the door, which in fact he had.

"Good evening, Bradley," said the comte to the old butler. "That was a singularly disgusting dinner."

"I am desolated it did not meet with your lordship's approval," said Bradley.

"Yes, but what are you going to *do* about it? Only see how spleenish these dreadful viands have made her ladyship."

"Jules. I must protest..."

"You see? Her ladyship protests also."

"And it please, my lord, Mrs. Hamilton, the cook, is very old and is due to retire from your lordship's employ."

"Good. Then you will spare Mrs. Hamilton's feelings by not repeating my criticisms. See Mr. Garnett and arrange that she be handsomely pensioned off. And find me a French chef."

"My lord, the only French chef I know of hereabouts belongs to Mr. and Miss Bryce-Connell."

"Is he accounted good?"

"Oh, excellent, my lord. Folks do say were it not for his artistry, then no one would call at the Bryce-Connells."

"I will lure him away. Thank you, Bradley."

When the butler left, Delphine said in a thin voice, "We did very well at Marsham Manor before you came. I was able to live a peaceful and well-ordered life. I have never had such an upsetting day. You chattered and chattered like a...a *chatterbox*. Sir George commanded respect from our neighbors. Oh, they have come to call, but simply because you are a freakish novelty."

"No one called on Sir George the Good."

"That was because he did not wish it so. Occasionally some of the French gentlemen he had rescued would visit us."

The comte looked surprised. "Although your French has much improved, my heart, you still speak our language with a correct English accent. I was under the impression that until the arrival of the Marquis de Graux and Monsieur Renaud you had not spoken to anyone French."

"That is correct."

"But if these people called, did you all speak in English?"

"I was not allowed to see them."

"Odso? Why?"

"Sir George felt the sight and sound of my countrymen might reanimate my memory and bring back to me the horrors I had endured."

"Rather short-sighted of him," murmured the comte. "Memory is a strange thing; the longer it is denied, the more violently it returns one day."

"Every word you say," said Delphine passionately, "is a criticism, direct or oblique, of Sir George Charteris. Well, I will never forget him, I will never stop admiring him."

"And neither you should," said the comte equably. "But do not expect to turn me into a copy of your late husband, Delphine."

"And why not? What better model could you have?"

"You know," he said plaintively, "some people might think I am rather a good sort of person myself."

"And no one more so than you yourself."

"Unfair, Delphine. All this bantering fatigues me immensely. You need not leave me to the seclusion of my port. I am going to retire."

"Then retire," shouted Delphine. "And good riddance!"

He looked at her for a long time, with a bland, pleasant expression in his blue eyes, until her own fell before his. Then he quietly left the room.

Delphine found her hands were trembling. She knew she had behaved abominably. But he disturbed her, threatened her peace by his very presence. He exuded a strong air of masculinity, a hint of possession. Today he had shown that he meant to be the master of Marsham Manor. That was not what troubled her.

There was something about him that suggested he was only biding his time, playing with her, until he should decide to master *her*.

And yet, on the other hand, she knew she had only to tell him she did not wish this marriage and he would leave.

After a long time, she became weary with her jumbled thoughts and decided to go to bed.

She went upstairs and slowly prepared for bed. She donned a very pretty nightgown of green silk with a deep décolletage and a froth of lace falling from the shoulders to the elbows. Delphine studied her reflection as she brushed out her hair. She had made the nightgown some years ago—why not admit it?—in the hope of making the staid and gentle Sir George more passionate.

The silk was very thin and showed every curve of her body.

She remembered the first time she had worn it, waiting for her husband, trembling in anticipation.

Sir George had entered the bedroom and had puttered about, getting ready for bed. Then he had seemed to see what she was wearing for the first time and had said, "Delphine, my angel, you must not wear such a thin and skimpy garment these winter nights." He had gone over to the chest of drawers and rummaged through them, finally drawing out a thick flannel nightdress.

"Now, put this on immediately," he had said in his fatherly way. "I do not wish you to catch the ague."

That had been the night that was to be one of many such nights, when Sir George had kissed her gently on the forehead before turning over and going to sleep.

During his last illness, he had insisted she take a suite of rooms for her own use.

Delphine looked at herself again and put down the brush with a sigh.

What would Jules think could he see her in it? she wondered suddenly.

She went and opened the window and rested her elbows on the sill.

It had been showery that day, and the air was fresh and cold, carrying the scent of cut grass and flowers. A light wind whispered restlessly in the trees, blowing a strand of Delphine's hair across her mouth.

And then she saw a dark figure lurking in the darkness of the trees at the edge of the lawns. Suddenly, the moon came out from behind its covering of cloud, and, at the same time, the figure stepped out from the shelter of the trees. It was a man with a thin, foxy face, white in the moonlight. He wore a drab sort of cloak and was hatless. He was watching the house intently.

Delphine drew back hurriedly and crossed the room and rang the bell. After some moments, a maid arrived, and Delphine told her there was an intruder in the grounds and to send out as many men as possible. Then she returned to the window. But of the mysterious intruder, there was no sign.

She stayed, watching, at the window as servants began to appear in the grounds carrying sticks and guns, torches and lanterns.

The matter was being taken care of, but Delphine had an urge to tell her husband about it. Of course, she was not going to his rooms so that he could see her in her green nightgown. Of course not! She was merely going to inform him of the reason for the commotion outside.

The comte had Sir George's old rooms, those that he had retired to in the last days of his illness. They were on the opposite side of the main staircase from those used by Delphine.

She knocked at his door and then went in, feeling silly and expecting him to be asleep.

But he was sitting by the fire, wrapped in a faded blue dressing gown which had seen better days.

"You really must order new clothes," said Delphine. "You must realize, Jules, that you may draw on the bank anytime you wish."

He rose to his feet and stood looking at her.

"*Ma foi*," he said wonderingly. "And you, my heart, should never wear anything else."

Delphine blushed. "I—I just came to tell you there was an intruder in the grounds. But I sent the servants to either find him or chase him away."

He was still staring at her, a warmth and a glow in his blue eyes she had not seen before.

"Jules!" said Delphine sharply. "You are not attending. There is an intruder in the grounds..."

He took two steps across the room and gathered her in his arms.

"Don't," begged Delphine. "Please don't."

He slid one hand up under her hair and put the other firmly in the small of her back and pressed her tightly against the length of his body.

She could feel a slow, rhythmic pulsation from his body, beating through her own. She told herself she should break away before he kissed her. But it was already too late.

His lips, hard and firm, were already covering her own, slowly softening as they caressed her mouth, parting her lips while one hand seductively stroked the nape of her neck and the other slid up between their bodies to close over her breast.

Delphine felt warm and drugged and languorous. His lazy, slow, sensual lovemaking was sweet and dizzying and infinitely pleasurable.

Then he swept her up into his arms, one hand sliding inside her nightgown, searching and teasing, while his mouth grew hard again, questioning, demanding. Her body sprang to frenzied life, aching, burning, yearning with frustration.

He took one step towards the bed.

"No!" screamed Delphine desperately.

And immediately she was put on her feet. Gentle, deft fingers arranged her slipping nightgown back on her shoulders. The comte settled himself comfortably in the armchair in front of the fire and opened his book again.

Delphine did not know what to do or say. She felt cold and sick and rejected. And yet she had *demanded* to be released with that cry of "No!"

With a stifled little sob, she turned and ran from the room.

She spent a tortured, restless night, plagued with longings to return to him, at other moments chiding herself for wishing to succumb to what was surely only base lust. It could not be love. You *respected* someone you loved. And she did not respect Jules. She fell asleep at last amid a tangle of blankets and sheets, not waking until ten o'clock the following morning, only to be told that Harriet Bryce-Connell had called and that his lordship had gone out riding with her.

Delphine waited for his return, wondering what on earth Harriet had been up to. Visions of the way those women, those wives of his clients, had looked at him began to flash through her mind.

At last she remembered it was the day of the coal and clothing club and took herself off to Littlejohn. At least he would not find her meekly waiting when he returned. Bradley had reported that there had been no trace of anyone in the grounds the night before although they had searched everywhere.

Probably a poacher, thought Delphine.

She rode towards Littlejohn through a fine, drizzling mist wondering what on earth her husband and Harriet could be doing, riding for all these hours on such a depressing day.

She made various calls on her tenants on the road back, spending more time with them than she usually did.

It was seven o'clock by the time she returned to Marsham Manor.

His lordship was in his rooms, Bradley informed her. He regretted he was too tired to dine with her ladyship but would see her in the morning. Mrs. Bencastle was dining in her room.

So that was that.

Delphine crossly ate her dinner in solitary splendor and then went up to bed, making as much noise as she could.

At last, she decided to call on him *before* she changed into her bedclothes. It was only polite to wish him good evening.

But this time, when she pushed open the door of his room, he was fast asleep, the moon shining in on his relaxed face.

Chapter Eight

❧

It was unusual for a hunt ball to be held in late spring, particularly when the Season was starting in London. But most of society was assembled around the Duke of Wellington in Brussels, and it was reported that London was vastly thin of company, so the hunt, in effect, was as good an excuse for a ball as any.

Maria Bencastle had, surprisingly, apologized to the comte for her malicious gossip. She had also freely apologized to everyone else. No one could quite understand the reason for this amazing about-face, but Delphine privately thought Maria had become tired of being so unpopular. Only look how happy and animated she had been since Sunday!

But the reason for Mrs. Bencastle's sweetness of demeanor was founded on the realization of a dream.

She would shortly have proof that the Comte Saint-Pierre was, in fact, a Bonapartist spy.

How she had found out this staggering piece of intelligence had come about like this.

Not wishing to stay cooped up at Marsham Manor in the company of the comte, and not wishing to brave any more indignities in Littlejohn, Maria decided to take the carriage over to the town of Hegsley on the far side of Littlejohn to attend morning service there.

The day was sunny and mild, and the service pleasantly soporific and dull.

Maria walked through the quiet Sunday streets of Hegsley, having left the carriage in the main square. She wanted to spend as much of the day away from Marsham Manor as possible. It had been infuriating to know that the comte had *not* been invited to Woburn and to have to keep quiet about it. For who in the surrounding county would believe anything she said now?

Attired in her grim mourning weeds, a black silhouette in the sunny, cobbled streets, Maria continued to wander aimlessly, like a bulldog searching for a lost bone.

She had reached the outskirts of the town, when she all at once espied the tall, green-coated figure of the comte. He was accompanied by a small, thin man with a very white, foxy face who was wrapped in a rusty brown cloak covered with travel stains.

They went into a small public house called the Green Man. Curiosity beginning to burn inside her, Maria waited a few moments and then quietly followed them in. The tap was empty except for the comte and his companion. She could not see them, but she could hear their voices.

They were seated at a table flanked by two high-backed settles. By seating herself at another sort of booth formed by this furniture arrangement directly behind them, Maria was able to overhear every word without being observed.

They had already ordered wine, and the landlord,

not having seen Maria enter, had retired to the back premises to eat his lunch.

Maria listened intently.

It transpired that the white-faced man was called Bodet.

To Maria's disappointment, they were talking in French. Then, to her relief, she heard the comte say sharply, "I would prefer to speak in English. French is not a very popular language these days. Why did you come to me with this information?"

"I happened to be in this area last week," said the man called Bodet, "and I heard it said that you were a supporter of Napoleon Bonaparte?"

There was a silence. "Isn't that lazy count going to say anything?" thought Maria. "He's probably gone to sleep."

Then the comte spoke. "And . . . ?" he prompted gently.

He had not denied it! Maria began to tremble with excitement.

"And so I came to beg your help, milord. I was placed in London a long time ago to pose as an *émigré*. While in London, I was to make my trade that of a hairdresser and ingratiate myself into the best households—which I did. When Napoleon was exiled on Elba, I thought my work was in vain, but word reached me to continue. And so I did."

"Continued what?"

"Arranging the hair of *les grandes dames* and searching through their husbands' papers."

"You were successful?"

"Not until a few weeks ago. At a certain general's house, I came across a portfolio in his study full of maps and plans and details of the strengths and weaknesses of the allies. I copied it carefully. I was not so stupid as to take it. *Alors,* my plan is to get these papers into the hands of Napoleon Bonaparte or one of his advisers."

"And what is stopping you?"

"I fear the authorities are suspicious of me. I had warning that my spying activities may have been discovered. Something about one of the maids having seen me sneak into the general's study when I was supposed to be on my way out of his house after arranging his wife's hair. I cannot risk being arrested at one of the ports. Then I heard about you. These stories about you are largely treated as rumor and gossip and will soon die away. In these country places, everyone French is suspect.

"But you now own English land through your marriage. You could easily get papers to pass over to France or Belgium without exciting much curiosity. All of the *beau monde* is in Brussels at the moment. There is hardly an English lord or lady left to grace the London Season."

"And what made *you* believe this gossip that I was a supporter of Napoleon?"

"Because I heard a great fat lady telling someone so, and the great fat lady who was all in black I discovered was none other than your wife's sister-in-law by her first marriage!"

"Ah, yes. That one."

"You will do this for me? The success of the emperor may depend on this information."

There was a long silence. A sound of clinking glasses came from the back. Maria prayed the landlord would not choose this moment to return.

"Yes," she heard the comte say. "I will do it."

"Bien!"

"But before I do, there is something you must do for me. Are you kept informed of the strength and movements and intentions of Napoleon's troops?"

"Yes, milord, I am kept well-informed."

"I would like you to meet me here next Friday and furnish me with all the details you can. That way, I will know exactly where to go. You must also give me a list of the names of the Bonapartist spies residing in London. Should the war continue for a long time, and if anything should happen to you, Bodet, I must know the names of my real friends among the French community in London."

"Such a list would be dangerous were it written down. I carry the names in my head."

"You must write them down or I shall not go."

Another silence.

"Very well," said Monsieur Bodet. "Next Friday, I will be here at the same time. And now, permit me to order another bottle to seal our bargain. Landlord!"

Maria slid quietly along the settle and, moving slowly and stealthily, gained the door of the inn without being seen.

Once out in the sunlight, she walked rapidly away, her heart beating hard.

Never had Maria Bencastle experienced such a feeling of elation.

Revenge would be very sweet indeed. She would pretend to be contrite over the cruel gossip she had spread. She would apologize to everybody. And then, on Thursday, she would alert the authorities. The inn at Hegsley would be surrounded, and the comte would be trapped with the incriminating evidence on him.

He would hang, and Delphine would mourn. But after a short time, things would go back to the way they had always been. She would stand by Delphine, and everyone would say what a marvelous, loyal, and Christian woman she was. Everyone would be sorry about how they had vilified her, and she would accept their apologies with touching modesty.

Delphine was driven to the hunt ball, which was to be held at Sir Giles Mancroft's mansion near Hegsley, by the comte. For all his retiring ways, the late Sir George had been an excellent judge of horseflesh and kept several carriages. The night was fine, so the comte was driving a smart racing curricle. Charlie was perched at the back, resplendent in his new livery. The little tiger had become a great favorite with the grooms and the coachman since he had an uncanny way with horses and could soon have the most recalcitrant feeding out of his hand.

Delphine was wearing her burgundy-colored silk gown with the worked embroidery of dull gold. She was wearing a heavy gold necklace set with emeralds around her neck and a gold and emerald circlet on her head. She had washed and brushed her curls and arranged them above the circlet in artistic disarray on top of her head.

The comte had mysteriously acquired new clothes. There had been no time to have them made, reflected Delphine. Perhaps he had found an unlucky gambler of his size among the local gentry. But somehow she could not ask him. It seemed too strange to ask one's husband where he managed to find his clothes.

He was resplendent in a green silk evening coat with a white waistcoat with silver embroidery, gold silk knee breeches, clocked stockings, and pumps with silver buckles. Delphine had given Bradley instructions to give the comte Sir George's jewel box. An emerald pin winked among the snowy folds of the comte's cravat, and emerald and diamond rings blazed on his fingers.

His hair was shining like newly minted gold under the curve of his curly brimmed beaver. He wore a many-caped driving coat and tan York gloves.

Delphine was warmly wrapped in a black velvet cloak lined with swansdown. It was late spring and the weather during the day had been fine, but the evening was chilly with great stars blazing in a black sky.

Although she was a twice-married matron and twenty-three years old, Delphine felt like a debutante. This was to be her first ball.

In trembling anticipation, she imagined the splendor of the ballroom, the glittering jewels, the light airs played by the orchestra, and the banks of hothouse flowers perfuming the air.

"I took it upon myself to pay for our tickets," said the comte, negotiating a turn in the road.

"*Pay* for our tickets!" exclaimed Delphine, startled. "But we were invited."

"That was a last-minute kindly gesture so that we would not feel left out, but I discovered everyone from Littlejohn and Hegsley will be there and they have all paid for their tickets. It seemed only correct to do the same."

"I did not know," said Delphine faintly.

"My informant was Mr. Partington, the haberdasher. Although the ball begins at eight o'clock, he said we should not be expected to arrive until after ten. *All* the plebeians, he assured me, arrive on time. The higher-ups deign to put in an appearance later."

"Oh," said Delphine in a small voice. "But we *are* going to be there at exactly eight o'clock."

"I considered it more courteous," said the comte with a smile. "Furthermore, I do not think you are the kind of lady who cares to make a grand entrance."

"Noooo . . ."

"And furthermore, Mr. Partington told me to please wear as many jewels as I could, which is why I am bedecked in your late husband's wealth. He said that last year everyone waited to see Lady Gladstone and her diamonds, and she did not turn up until quite midnight and without a single jewel. The evening was accounted uncommonly flat as a consequence."

"I—I hope I can dance," said Delphine nervously.

"Have you not been taught?"

"I had a dancing instructor, but perhaps it will not be quite the same thing in a room full of people."

"It should be no different."

The road all at once seemed to be full of a great deal of traffic. There were flies and chaises and traps and other carriages of every description. Even Hegsley's

129

last two remaining sedan chairs were in service, the town's elderly chairmen scurrying along as fast as they could with their burdens so that they might be in time to return to Hegsley and pick up other fares.

Delphine began to relax. It was not going to be a stately ball with only the upper crust of the county, after all. And perhaps she would have practiced enough to perform her steps properly before Harriet Bryce-Connell arrived.

Sir Giles Mancroft's home was a rather shabby, rambling house grandly called Mancroft Towers. It had originally been a small Elizabethan manor, and subsequent periods of architecture seemed to have been added at random.

The ballroom was one of the most modern additions, having been stuck on to the back of the house in the 1790s. Delphine left her cloak in the cloakroom, joined her husband, who was waiting for her in the hall, and then both made their way through a series of twists and turns to the ballroom.

The seats for the aristocracy were on a sort of dais at the far end of the room, directly under the musicians' gallery.

The ballroom had been decorated by the young ladies of Hegsley and Littlejohn with more enthusiasm than expertise. Branches of evergreen hung drunkenly from the gilt frames of looking glasses and shrouded the marble mantel over the fireplace. All sorts of vases were bursting with the flowers of field and garden and had been placed in awkward spots and were balanced precariously on wobbly pedestals.

Sir Giles Mancroft was a small, wizened man wearing a bag wig and green spectacles. His wife was enormous and square, with a small, pretty face and neat features. She looked as if she had borrowed someone else's body for a joke.

The comte promptly led Lady Mancroft out to where

a set was forming for a country dance. Sir Giles croakingly apologized to Delphine, explaining that his rheumatism prevented him from performing.

After some hesitation and much whispering, the bookseller from Littlejohn, Mr. Harry Withers, a fresh-faced young man, shyly asked Delphine if she would honor him with a dance.

Delphine accepted and nervously took her place in the set while the tinny orchestra crashed into the opening strains of "Monymusk."

Poor Delphine muttered instructions to herself under her breath as she tried to master the complications of "Cross hands and back again, down the middle and up again." But she was constantly snatching hold of the wrong hands, and apologizing, and tripping over feet as she tried to find the right partner. Then when she returned to her place, she made the mistake of stopping, quite forgetting that she was supposed to go on capering until she reached the bottom of the set.

But the delight of the tradespeople at the spectacle of Delphine and the comte taking the floor was beyond bounds. Lady Mancroft had *never* before been known to dance until the aristocracy arrived in force.

Their delight and goodwill were infectious. How manfully and gallantly did the bookseller blame all Delphine's clumsiness on himself!

By the end of the dance, however, Delphine had fully resolved to sit against the wall for the rest of the evening.

But Mr. Partington requested the pleasure of her company in the quadrille, looking at her with pleading eyes, terrified that he would have to turn around and walk back down the length of the dance floor with everyone knowing he had been rejected.

Delphine accepted.

Mr. Partington was so terrified at the honor being done him that he stumbled and staggered through the dance, until Delphine, too concerned for him to worry about herself, found she was performing her own steps very competently, and from that moment on, she began to enjoy herself.

Next she danced a Scotch reel with her husband, laughing and breathless as they whirled about.

Dance followed dance until, at half-past ten, the doors at the end of the ballroom opened, and Harriet Bryce-Connell, her brother, Lady Gladstone, Sir Frederic Gibson, the lord-lieutenant, Lady Gibson, the Earl and Countess of Hollingford and their daughters, Lady Clara and Lady Lucy, and the Honorable John and Mrs. Caxford made their entrance.

Formerly, all the plebeians would stop dancing when the grand folk arrived and bow and curtsy while they made their majestic progress to the end of the room.

But this year it was different. They had the comte dancing with the butcher's wife and Delphine dancing with the baker, and so the uppercrust of the county had to edge their way around the edge of the floor instead of marching straight down the middle.

At last, they surrounded the Mancrofts, exclaiming at the Saint-Pierres' *democracy,* "but after all they *are* French and do not know how to go on."

But Sir Giles would have none of it. So far, he said, it had been the best hunt ball yet.

In previous years, the tradespeople had waited so that they might have a glimpse of the aristocracy before going home, sometimes having to wait as late as midnight and worrying about the amount of coal and candles it was costing back home, since their domestics were waiting up for them.

Mothers would worry about children who were probably not yet abed. This year, however, they had not only had the pleasure of seeing the comte and comtesse from the very start but of dancing with them, too. Sir Giles and Lady Mancroft were warm in their praise.

With great daring, it had been planned that the waltz

would be introduced for the first time. Of course, everyone had practiced it in secret for quite some time, but it had always been considered too forward a dance for a country ball.

The waltz was announced. Delphine had never learned the steps but was so pleased with her dancing success so far, that she was confident of picking up the steps very quickly if her husband would guide her.

But the comte was talking to Harriet, a Harriet resplendent in white muslin worked with silver thread and a diamond necklace and tiara. She looked like a fairy princess, her eyes as blue as the comte's, her hair as gold.

Mr. Caxford asked Delphine to dance. Delphine looked anxiously towards her husband and murmured that she had not learned the steps, whereupon Mr. Caxford promptly asked Lady Lucy.

The comte took the floor with Harriet.

Bitterly Delphine watched as her husband held Harriet in a firm clasp. Harriet seemed to float in his arms.

"By Jove! What a marvelous couple they make!" exclaimed Sir Giles, forgetting Delphine's presence.

To Delphine, the waltz was a shameless dance and went on much too long.

At last it was over, but the comte promenaded with his fair partner, as was the custom.

Since everyone knew Harriet to be monstrously high in the instep, no other partner came up to claim her hand for the next dance. Delphine was again asked by the bookseller, and accepted, noticing out of the corner of one jaundiced eye her husband leading Harriet into the refreshment room. Harriet was leaning against him in a disgustingly familiar way and batting her eyelashes, which were surely darkened with lamp black.

It was a long time before they reappeared, and when they did, Harriet was flushed and elated, and the comte looked like a cat that had just had a large bowl of cream.

He asked Delphine to partner him in a country dance

and she angrily refused, whereupon he turned and asked Harriet to dance again.

Delphine took the floor with the vicar.

Would this awful evening never end?

Jules's admiration of Harriet was becoming more blatant by the minute. Harriet looked cool and fresh as well she might—*she* had not been dancing for hours.

At last the ball finished.

It was a silent ride home, on Delphine's part at least.

Her infuriating husband chattered on about what fun it had all been, and how jolly the people were, and how friendly.

Delphine sat and scowled out into the night. A vision of the pink and blond Harriet seemed to dance in front of her eyes with every movement of the carriage. Tears pricked at Delphine's eyelids. This husband, this Frenchman, had made her feel more foreign than ever. She felt sallow and dark and dowdy.

On arriving at Marsham Manor, the comte promptly plunged into a long and enthusiastic discussion of horseflesh with Charlie. Delphine stood on the steps for a few moments watching them, then turned on her heel and walked inside and straight up to her bedroom.

After she had changed into a simple, unadorned, white cambric nightgown, she brushed her hair with swift, angry strokes. She was not jealous of Harriet. She could *not* be!

She faintly heard Jules mounting the stairs and put down the brush and listened hard. But when had he ever come to her room?

Delphine choked back an angry sob. She snuffed the candles one by one and climbed into bed and buried her face in the pillow.

She was so angry she thought she would not sleep, but the fatigue of the evening's dancing had been great, and it was three in the morning, so she plunged down into the realm of dreams almost immediately.

All at once, she was in her mother's arms. She could

smell her faint rose perfume and feel the trembling of her body. They were at the château window.

"Kill me!" screamed her mother desperately. "Kill me, but save my child."

A great roar of derision came from the mob below, and flames started to shoot up, scarlet and yellow crackling flames, lighting up the avid, staring faces below.

"*Maman!*" wailed Delphine. "*Maman!*"

The comte had gone downstairs again to look for a book.

He turned over volume after volume. Mostly books on agriculture. He tugged at a copy of *Tristram Shandy*, glad to find something readable, and as he pulled it from the shelves, a fat volume of *The Pig Breeders' Almanac* fell to the floor. The pages flew open, and a pressed and dried pink rose floated to his feet.

He bent, slowly and carefully picking it up, a tender smile curling his lips. He remembered Delphine as she had been at the fair; beautiful, alive, slightly arrogant, slightly contemptuous of the poor performer who could dress and speak like a gentleman yet earned his living in such a low way.

He placed the flower back in the book and closed the pages. Picking up the copy of *Tristram Shandy*, he made his way back into the hall and up the stairs.

He was about to turn off at the landing towards his own quarters when he heard his wife scream.

He ran lightly to her bedroom and pushed open the door and hurtled in.

"*Maman!*" said Delphine, her voice strange and piping, the voice of a frightened child.

He lit a branch of candles and sat down on the bed and gathered her tightly in his arms.

"Wake up, my heart," he whispered urgently. "You are dreaming."

Delphine awoke and stared up at him, her eyes haunted with dreams.

"The fire," she whispered. "And the faces, the horrible, staring faces!"

"Shhh!" he said, rocking her. "You are safe. You are here with me."

Delphine gave a great shuddering sob and buried her face against his chest. He stroked her hair gently. "It is as well to remember," he said softly. "After a time, the horrors begin to fade. So many of us have been through so much."

Delphine raised her wet eyes to his. "You, too?"

"It was part of their sport," he said, "to make me stand and watch my parents being beheaded. They knew I was there. They were very brave. I lived with fear for a long time, fear and terrible nightmares. But we are alive, Delphine, and we are together. We have each other."

Delphine clung to him, listening to his calm voice and hearing the steady beating of his heart.

"I have not been very kind to you, Jules," she said.

"Perhaps not. I was not the man of your dreams."

He brushed away a tear on her cheek with one finger and smiled down into her eyes. Delphine's dropped shyly before his gaze. He seemed to be wearing nothing but his old dressing gown. The firm column of his throat was very close to her lips, the skin smooth and white.

He shifted slightly on the bed, and she grasped the lapels of his dressing gown and said on a note of panic, "Do not leave me!"

"I can go on holding you for a little, and comforting you, but you are not a child, Delphine. Already, I am all too aware of your body—and your beauty."

"I am not so beautiful as Harriet," mumbled Delphine.

"Much more beautiful," he teased. "Unlike Harriet,

136

you are beautiful inside as well as out. Did I make you jealous this evening? I tried very hard."

"Oh, *that's* why . . . oh, *Jules* how wicked you are."

"Your lips are swollen and red and ripe for the plucking, my sweeting. But what if I kiss you now and you cry 'no'?"

Delphine looked at him tremulously. She was not a virgin, but she felt slightly frightened, slightly insecure, afraid of turning him cold by her lack of experience.

She raised one shaking little hand and traced the contours of his lips. "I would not cry 'no,'" she said.

He bent his head and kissed her long and lingeringly, using only the movement of his mouth against hers to make love to her until he felt the quickening of her heartbeat and noticed the hot color rising in her face.

His hand reached for the sash of his dressing gown.

"The candles," said Delphine. "Blow them out."

"Very well, my love. But do not forget for one moment who holds you in his arms."

He blew out the candles. Delphine moved over on the bed, listening to the rustle of silk as he removed his dressing gown.

And then he was in bed beside her. He eased her nightgown over her head and threw it on the floor.

"I *cannot*," said Delphine in sudden panic. "I am too afraid."

He silenced her with his mouth and began to stroke the length of her body, pressing her against him, until at long last he felt her begin to relax. His kisses became fiercer and more insistent, and when his mouth began to trace an erotic path down her body, she buried her hands in his hair and gave herself up to the thudding tumult of emotion engulfing her.

By the time he took her, she was ready for him, meeting passion with passion, twisting and turning under him, each thrust of his body sending her spiraling up higher and higher until she seemed to collapse all of a sudden, down and down into a warm, black sea of content. But still he had not finished with her, bringing her back to those dizzying heights three times before he joined her, culminating their lovemaking in one long and glorious fiery frenzy that left them both shipwrecked on the shores of love after such a long storm of passion.

Delphine awoke in the light of a red dawn, and he immediately came awake as well, his mouth sleepily seeking hers and his body beginning to move against hers.

"Oh, Jules." Delphine giggled. "You are not lazy *at all*," and then that was the last coherent thing Delphine was to say for some time.

When she awoke again, the sun was high in the sky and the comte was gone.

Delphine felt like a child at Christmas. The whole glorious day stretched before her, a day she would spend by her husband's side.

She sang as she washed and put on a sprigged muslin gown.

She could never remember being so happy.

Delphine ran lightly down the stairs.

And stopped on the first landing, her hand flying to her mouth.

The comte was standing in a shaft of sunlight in the hall; Harriet Bryce-Connell was held in his arms. They were kissing passionately.

Delphine turned and ran back to her room, a black roaring in her ears.

All the glory and beauty of the night had meant nothing to him. Perhaps he was even now laughing with Harriet over the ingenuousness of his bride.

She sat on the edge of the bed and clutched her head in her hands.

She *hated* Jules, hated him as she had never hated anyone in her life before.

There came a gentle scratching at the door, and she turned white as his voice called, "Are you awake?"

Delphine had locked the door. She sat silently, watching as the handle turned.

"Delphine!" His voice was sharper. "Let me in. The door is locked."

"I am going to sleep for another hour or two," Delphine forced herself to call out. "Farmer Yardley wanted to see me about something. Would you ride over there instead? I will be waiting for you when you return."

"Very well, sleepyhead." He sounded amused. "I will see you very soon."

Delphine waited until she heard him go back downstairs. She waited, rigid, until she heard him drive away.

And then she rang the bell.

The servants were thrown into an uproar. Her ladyship announced her intention of leaving for London *immediately*. One of the housemaids, Jane, was told she was to accompany her mistress.

Trunks were packed and corded at great speed; the traveling carriage was brought around. Charlie ran hither and thither, asking questions and getting no answers.

Maria Bencastle had gone into Littlejohn. Delphine left her a curt note to say she wished to see some of the shops and theaters in London and would be gone several weeks. Then she pulled forward another piece of paper and began to write to her husband.

> *"Jules. My lapse into the stews of lust last night has somewhat sickened me. I have decided we will not suit. Do not try to follow me to London. When I return, I hope we will be able to discuss the dissolution of our marriage. The whole thing has been a Most Disastrous Mistake. D."*

She told Bradley to deliver it to the comte when he returned.

Mr. Yardley's farm lay well away from the London road.

Dry-eyed and bitter and hard-faced, Delphine sat bolt upright as the carriage rolled away from Marsham Manor.

Jane, the little maid, a sunny-natured girl with a fresh country complexion and mop of black curls, opened her mouth to say something, but the grim look on her mistress's face made her change her mind.

Coldly, Delphine made plans. She would find a suite of rooms in a reputable hotel, and then let her lawyers find her a townhouse and see about engaging a temporary staff for what was left of the Season.

She would visit as many of London's amusements as she could, so long as they did not involve seeing one member of the French community.

She wanted to forget she had ever been French. And most of all, she wanted to forget that ruthless and callous heartbreaker, the Comte Saint-Pierre.

Chapter Nine

❖

Maria Bencastle was in a state of high excitement. The only thing to mar her pleasure was the absence of Delphine. How strange to have taken off for London just like that! But once all this was over, Maria meant to find her. Someone would have to break the sad news to Delphine, and who better than she?

What a terrible job she had had to persuade the magistrate that Jules Saint-Pierre was a spy! But at last, she had enlisted the aid of Geoffrey Bryce-Connell and his sister, Harriet. For some reason, Harriet was most bitter about the comte and in a receptive mood to hear any bad news about him. Her brother was in the same frame of mind, since he had been told by his chef that that worthy was leaving to take up employment at Marsham Manor. They had listened avidly to her story and then had taken her to see the lord-lieutenant of the county, Sir Frederic Gibson. After that, things had started to happen rapidly.

Now she was waiting in a closed carriage with Harriet and Geoffrey on the outskirts of Hegsley, where they could see the entrance to the Green Man. Closing in along the surrounding lanes were the members of the Bedfordshire Yeomanry, led by Colonel Arburthnot.

"I hope this isn't more of your silly gossip, Maria," said Harriet suddenly. "Perhaps we should not have listened to you."

"Look," said Maria. "What do you think of my silly gossip now?"

The foxy-faced man had entered the inn some ten minutes before. Looking in that direction, following the line of Maria's black-mittened hand, Harriet and Geoffrey saw the tall figure of the comte, strolling along the quiet village street.

They were too busy staring at him to notice the small figure of a sweep, laden under his brushes and poles, going into the inn ahead of the comte.

Maria licked her lips.

"They will give the traitor a moment to collect the papers and then they will have him," she whispered. "I *told* Delphine the man was..."

"Shut up!" hissed Harriet. "That voice of yours carries for miles."

But no one could have said anything to Maria Bencastle which would upset her during this, her moment of triumph.

Inside the inn, the comte quietly studied the papers which Monsieur Bodet had handed him. Then he gave a nod. "I am surprised at some of these names," he said grimly.

"And I am surprised you did not know they were supporters of our emperor," said Monsieur Bodet sharply.

"You forget," said the comte with a bitter smile. "Despite Mrs. Bencastle's gossip, I was not a spy, only a sympathizer. I did not talk politics in London, you know. I was too concerned in making my living."

"As long as I can be sure of your loyalty," said Monsieur Bodet, squinting up at him.

"My dear fellow," said the comte languidly, "I would hardly be offering to carry such dangerous material to France were I not a very ardent supporter of Napoleon. I trust he will restore my estates in return for me risking my life?"

"Of course," said Monsieur Bodet with a private sneer. These *aristos* were all the same, he thought. They would join any side just so long as they could get their precious estates back. But the familiar reason, the familiar plea, reassured him.

"I hope our voices do not carry," he whispered. "It seems as if that sweep is paying more attention to our conversation than to his work."

The comte glanced over to where the small sweep was joining up his poles ready to attack the inn fireplace. The landlord was nowhere in sight.

The comte rose to his feet. "It seems we must serve ourselves," he said, fetching a bottle of wine and two glasses. "The place seems deserted. Well, Monsieur Bodet, drink a glass with me and wish me Godspeed."

"The emperor!" said Monsieur Bodet, draining his glass in one gulp.

He reached for the bottle to fill his glass again. "You did not drink the toast," he said, looking at the comte's still full glass. "You..."

His eyes widened, and he made an effort to rise. "You tricked me," he croaked, "the papers..."

The papers were lying on the table in front of the comte. Bodet made a grab for them, and the comte whipped them up and put them in his pocket.

Bodet fell full length across the table and lay still.

"Poisoned 'im, 'ave yer?" asked the sweep.

"No, Charlie," said the comte without turning around.

"I've drugged him. What on earth are you doing with a black face?"

"The military's closing in," said Charlie urgently. "That Maria Bencastle's hiding in a carridge outside wiff the Bryce-Connell lot. Looks like a trap. Here, you ain't a traitor, are you?"

"No, Charlie."

"Well, can't you tell them, like?"

"No. By the time they believed me, *if* they believed me, it might be too late."

"It nearly *is* too late," said Charlie. "I thought you was up to somethin' you wouldn't want anyone to know abaht. Here, black your phiz and cover yourself up wiff this dirty great cloak and take me poles."

"Do you think it will work?"

"Surely. When did a body ever look close at a sweep?"

Quickly the comte blacked his face with soot from the fireplace. He swung a ragged, burned cloak over his clothes.

"Yer hair's too bright," said Charlie. "Here!"

He pulled a dirty hat and kerchief out of his sack. Soon the comte's gold curls were extinguished.

Charlie jerked a thumb in the direction of the sleeping Frenchman. "Wot abaht 'im?"

"Leave him," said the comte. "I meant to give him to the authorities, but since they are already here, they will find him."

"Someone's coming out of the inn," hissed Maria. "Are they going to take all day?"

"Relax," said Harriet. "Here comes the brave colonel and his men."

They watched while the colonel and one of his officers walked up to the inn.

"They're talking to those two sweeps," said Geoffrey.

All watched while the taller of the sweeps nodded

to the colonel and jerked his thumb in the direction of the inn they had just left.

The colonel pressed a coin into the taller sweep's grimy hand and then waved his arm. The yeomanry began to creep towards the inn from the side streets until it was surrounded. The two sweeps strolled off down the street, chatting easily, and occasionally turning to look behind them.

Then, at another signal from Colonel Arburthnot, his troops stormed the inn.

Maria opened the carriage door and stepped down. This was her moment of triumph. When he was dragged from the inn by the soldiers, she wanted to make sure that the first face the comte saw was her own.

There was a long silence.

The townspeople had been alerted and everyone was indoors. Curtains twitched, smoke rose lazily to the clear blue sky from cottage chimneys, far away a dog barked.

Then the inn door burst open, and Colonel Arburthnot shot out into the street.

"Those sweeps!" he shouted. "Find them."

"Oh, lor'," came Harriet's tinkling voice. "How *stoopid*! Those sweeps. I declare it must have been Jules and probably that tiger of his. And Arburthnot gave him money!"

She began to laugh and laugh while Maria's face grew as black as her clothes.

She was consumed with rage. He had escaped.

But one thing was certain. All the world would now know him for the spy he was.

Soldiers carried out the drugged body of Monsieur Bodet and walked off down the street. The rest spread out, searching for the two sweeps, calling on the townspeople to come out and help.

All the long day they searched. But of the Comte Saint-Pierre and his tiger, Charlie, there was not the slightest sign.

"Well, that was all very disappointing," said Harriet, yawning, as the carriage bearing her, her brother, and Maria rolled slowly homeward in the early evening twilight through the country lanes leading to Littlejohn.

As the carriage passed through the main square of Littlejohn, Geoffrey Bryce-Connell suddenly rapped on the roof of the coach with his cane. "Stop, I say," he called to his coachman.

"What *is* the matter, Geoffrey?" said Harriet wearily. "I want to go home."

"What on earth is that Partington chap putting up in his shop window?" said Geoffrey. The carriage pulled alongside the haberdashery shop and rolled to a stop.

With tears running down his face, Mr. Partington was pasting a huge notice on the window of his shop. It said:

THIS ESTABLISHMENT IS LOYAL TO THE COMTE SAINT-PIERRE AND DOES NOT BE-LIEVE ONE WORD OF THE WICKED SLAN-DERS AND LIES ABOUT HIM THAT HAVE BEEN PUT ABOUT.

Maria Bencastle gasped.

"Poor Maria," murmured Harriet. "I really don't think all your great efforts are going to make you the teensiest bit more popular. Do you?"

The Battle of Waterloo was finally over. The allies, headed by the great Duke of Wellington, had defeated Napoleon Bonaparte.

Jules Saint-Pierre sat at a country inn outside Brussels with his tiger, Charlie, and wondered whether to return to England or to go on to Paris and offer his services to the restored king, Louis XVIII. It was good to be away from the terrible scenes of death and disease which still haunted Brussels.

The evening was golden and still. They were seated

at a small table outside the inn, watching the sun going down over the fields at the end of the town.

"I thought they would've given you a uniform, guv," said Charlie plaintively. "You know, one of them like the prince regent wears, all gold and stars and things."

"I was not out of place, Charlie," said the comte, looking down ruefully at his battle-stained morning coat. "There was not time, and a great number of the officers were even wearing evening dress, having gone straight from the Duchess of Richmond's ball."

He had delivered the information he had collected from Bodet about the strength and position of Napoleon's troops to the Duke of Wellington's staff before the battle. The information stolen from the general by Bodet he had left at Horse Guards in London, before leaving for Belgium.

"Do you fink they'll fink...think...you're a spy back at Marsham?" asked Charlie.

"I shouldn't think so. The kind gentlemen at the Horse Guards sent off a letter to the lord-lieutenant telling him of my help."

"Didn't it feel funny fighting them French, I mean being French yourself?"

"I was fighting a tyrant. That was all I thought." The comte sighed. "My poor people, all those poor soldiers, English and French alike. I never thought to get the stink of gangrene out of my nostrils again. Never will I forget the fields of Waterloo and the terrible harvest of dead bodies, fields and fields of them."

"Are we going to Paris?"

"My adopted regiment has already gone, what's left of them. I do not think, apart from my commanding officers, they quite knew who I was. I joined, I fought, I stayed alive, and you stayed with me right through it. I'm proud of you Charlie. You're a Trojan."

Charlie's wizened little cockney face turned pink with pleasure.

"It makes you fi...think," he said, striving as usual

to emulate his master's upper-crust tones. "It makes you wonder about Marsham and how they all are. Quiet there it was, guv. Luverley and quiet, like. All them horses. I used to sit in the stables of a morning wiff the sun coming in at the door and feel as 'appy as . . . as anything. We ain't going back?"

"I fear we would not be welcome."

"Didn't you tell her, then?"

"Tell who . . . what?"

"Why, the missus, guv."

"What are you talking about, man?"

"Well, see here," said Charlie awkwardly. "There waren't time to go into it, like. You see, I saw that Mrs. Bencastle leaving, and she looked at me with a kind of *gloating* look. So I ups and hangs on the back-strap o' her carriage. She only had one groom driving, James, it was, but no other servants. She goes right to them Bryce-Connells and sends the carriage home. I crept up to the windows but could only hear a bit but it was enuff. She was sayin' somethin' about, 'Now, I have him. He's at the Green Man at Hegsley,' and then I couldn't hear no more.

"I pinches a horse from their stables and rode into Littlejohn and saw the sweep and gave him a crown to let me have his duds for the day. Then I rode to Hegsley, and the rest you know. I knew you was in trouble, so I thought I'd best bring a disguise for you as well. We've had to run so many times, guv, but usually from the duns. Nearly knocked me flat when I thought you was a spy."

"Yes, yes! You have told me all this a hundred times. But what didn't you have time to tell me?"

"I was waitin' in the hall for you the morning before that, case you wanted me, when that Miss Bryce-Connell sails in and plants a kiss right smack on your mouff, and there's the missus standing up on the landing looking like she'd been shot. But arter you had told that Harriet woman that you loved your wife and all that and she had raged off, I sees you go up the stairs, and then you comes down whistling and says you're off to Farmer Yardley. So I thought, that's all right. Then the missus leaves, and I tried to say something and you yells at me to shut my phiz, so I did, but I thought I'd tell you next day what she'd seen, but by that time I was too busy finding out wot Mrs. Bencastle had in mind."

"Do you mean her ladyship thought that I . . . ?"

"Well, if you didn't explain nothin' to her, guv, then it must have looked right bad."

The comte struck his fist on the table, sending the glasses rattling.

"That's it!" he said. "That is why she left me that disgusting note."

Charlie watched him with bright eyes.

"So where are we going, guv?"

"Home, Charlie. London first. She may still be there."

"Home, it is." Charlie grinned.

Delphine had been living for over a month in a trim house on Berkeley Street that was owned by a family who had followed the ton to Brussels and had moved on to Paris after the victory at Waterloo and were not expected to return until August.

Since it came at a modest rent, fully furnished and with a resident staff of servants, all Delphine had had to do was move in and take up residence.

She was using her previous married name and was known to society as Lady Charteris. Maria Bencastle had been unable to find her, since Delphine had left strict instructions with her lawyers and servants that her address was not to be given to anyone.

Delphine had written to Maria, however, urging that lady to find herself a new home as soon as possible. For Delphine had heard all about the comte's spying activities. The fact that it had been discovered he was spying for the English and not the French had not yet reached her ears. Mr. Garnett, the steward, had assumed the lord-lieutenant had written to her, and the lord-lieutenant had assumed her husband had kept her informed of events, and so she was left in miserable ignorance.

The news that Jules was a French spy was somehow a confirmation of all her worst fears about him.

It underlined his shameless behavior with Harriet. She had been tricked. That was all. Life must go on.

But to return to Marsham meant to return to memories of him, and so Delphine stayed on in town.

She had hired an elderly dowager, Mrs. Castle, as companion and chaperone. Mrs. Castle was the complete opposite of Maria Bencastle. She was a middle-aged lady with a great deal of vivacity and a frivolous mind. She lived for fashion and pleasure. She did not know of Delphine's second marriage and assumed she was a widow.

Mrs. Castle had short skirts on her gowns and false curls on her forehead and never stopped talking. But she was amiable and uncritical, and her endless energy kept Delphine busy on a round of calls and engagements.

Delphine had become very fashionable in appearance. Mrs. Castle had no taste in dress when it came to herself but seemed to know to a nicety how to set off Delphine's dark and vital good looks.

One by one, Delphine had begun to gather a small court of admirers. They were mostly gentlemen without any serious intentions, gentlemen who liked to be seen courting, and so she enjoyed their company without ever having to worry about any relationship developing into anything deeper.

Mrs. Castle's rouged and wrinkled face would sometimes crease up in perplexity over Delphine's choice of gallants. Lady Charteris seemed to go out of her way to encourage men who did not want to get married and shunned those who did.

Delphine refused to read the newspapers and seemed totally uninterested in reports of the famous Battle of Waterloo.

The fact was she did not want to read anything that might remind her of her husband's betrayal of his adopted country.

But it seemed that celebrations of the battle were everywhere. At Astley's Royal Amphitheatre in Lambeth, Delphine sat with the spectators and watched a reproduction of the village of Quatre Bras being shown "partly by moonlight and partly by torchlight and firelight."

And at Vauxhall Pleasure Gardens at ten o'clock in the evening, the famous battle was staged with a thousand men and two hundred horses in action, a great deal of gunpowder and shot, and a scenic display which sent the French up in flames, much to the delight of the English audience.

Delphine tried very hard not to think of the comte at all, for, if she did, she saw him through the distorting glass of her hurt. His handsome face became weak, his curls brassy, and his manners posturing and effete.

One evening, she set out for Vauxhall with her current escort, Mr. Jeremy Heaton, a tall young man who hardly said a word, and Mrs. Castle. Vauxhall was not so fashionable as it had been, but it still drew a vast number of pleasure seekers of all ranks of society. Its illuminated grounds were a great attraction. Thousands of little colored lamps decorated the trees and the triumphal arches, and flimsy pavilions glittered in the evening air above cascades of water and romantic sylvan grottos.

Much squealing and squalling was heard from the girls who ventured into the notorious Dark Walk in the hope of being ambushed by some of the gay bloods who were hanging about for just that purpose. There were fireworks, tumblers, rope dancers, singers, Indian jugglers, and sword swallowers to provide entertainment, and geegaws to be bought at rackety prices.

Mrs. Castle felt that her young friend was a great deal too interested in all the vulgar performers who crowded the gardens, and was amazed when Delphine's eyes filled with tears at the sight of a young man juggling balls.

Delphine appeared content at first to sit in the box hired for the evening by Mr. Heaton, sipping rack punch and watching the colorful passersby.

"Aren't some of these ladies, if one can call them ladies, quite shameless?" exclaimed Mrs. Castle, putting up her glass and staring through it with one snapping black eye at a rouged and painted female who was shrieking with laughter and ogling all the boxes.

"I really think Vauxhall has become too—how shall I put it?—*demi-mondaine*," Mrs. Castle continued. "People stare so. Now, do but look at that funny little creature with the straw sticking in his mouth. Quite like an ostler. I declare he cannot take his eyes off you."

Delphine idly glanced to where Mrs. Castle was pointing with her fan, and her face went rigid.

"Charlie," she whispered.

"Charlie!" exclaimed Mrs. Castle. "You *know* that creature?"

"Some servant who used to work for me," said Delphine, turning her head away.

Charlie approached until he was standing under the box.

"Shooo!" said Mrs. Castle, flapping her fan. "Be off with you."

"Missus!" said Charlie coaxingly. "Please listen to me, missus."

"Hey, what's amiss?" said Mr. Heaton, rousing himself from his usual silent torpor. He looked from Del-

152

phine's averted face down to Charlie's impudent, wrinkled one and stood up.

"Be off with you, fellow," he said. "Here!" Mr. Heaton looked around for help. "This fellow is making a nuisance of himself."

When he looked back, Charlie had gone.

Delphine was very white. "I must go home," she said, getting abruptly to her feet.

"But we have only arrived!" said Mrs. Castle. "But you do look so white. Did that horrible man frighten you? Was he sent off without a character? Did he *steal* the silver?"

"No, *no*, nothing like that," said Delphine in a trembling voice. "It's simply my head aches so."

Mrs. Castle chattered the whole way home, speculating on Charlie's imaginary crimes. Then she insisted on following Delphine up to her bedchamber and fussing about, ringing bells and demanding a hot posset for Delphine to drink and burnt feathers to be held under her nose.

"Don't chatter and fuss so," snapped Delphine at last. "Just go away!"

And at that, Mrs. Castle, who had never heard a harsh word before from Delphine, burst into tears and turned faint and ended up drinking the hot posset and having feathers burnt under *her* nose. By the time the companion's lacerated feelings had been soothed and she had finally been persuaded to leave, Delphine felt exhausted.

The room felt hot and stuffy, and she pushed up the window and took a great gulp of warm, sooty London air.

If Charlie were in London, then it followed that Jules must be in London as well.

Did he ever think of her?

Should she tell the authorities that his accomplice, Charlie, had been spotted, and have them both arrested?

It was her duty.

A carriage full of noisy bloods clattered down the street, their drunken voices raised in song.

They saw Delphine at the window and began to shout and exclaim. Delphine shut the window firmly, planning to open it again when they had gone.

She did not notice the small figure of the tiger moving back into the shadows across the street.

Delphine now had a lady's maid, Baxter, who came in at that moment and stood ready to help her mistress prepare for bed.

"Leave me, Baxter," said Delphine wearily. "I will put myself to bed. Tell the other servants to go to bed, also. I will not be needing anything else."

When the maid had gone, Delphine opened the window again and sat in a chair next to it, listening to the night sounds of London. The harsh voice of the watch said it was eleven o'clock and a starry night.

Eleven! It seemed so early to Delphine, who had become accustomed to going to bed at dawn.

There were further wild sounds of drunken roistering from the street below. The sounds became louder and louder and then gradually faded away as the revelers passed below.

It was then that Delphine became aware of the strange rumbling sounds from the chimney.

She started to her feet and stared at the fireplace. Was there some great bird trapped in the chimney? Was there about to be some gigantic fall of soot? That had happened before. Soot had cascaded into the room with a soft *thuck*, blackening her and everything in the bedroom. But the chimneys had all been cleaned since then.

The noises grew louder. Just as Delphine was about to ring the bell, there was an almighty crash, and a small black figure staggered out of the fireplace and landed on the hearth.

Delphine's first emotion was one of pity, not fear.

It must be some poor little climbing boy who had been trapped in the flue, and had just managed to get down.

A choked voice emerged from the blackened figure.

"Missus," it said plaintively.

"Charlie!" Delphine reached for the bell.

"Don't," said Charlie desperately. "You've got to listen to me."

"I do not listen to traitors and spies," said Delphine, her eyes filling with tears of shock.

"Wot you talkin' abaht?" said Charlie hotly. "The guv ain't no spy. He's a *hero*. He fought all them Frenchies at Waterloo. Didn't nobody *tell* you nuffin?"

Delphine sat down weakly. "What are you talking about, Charlie? The last I heard, your master was branded as a spy and a traitor. Maria wrote me such a dreadful letter through my lawyers telling me all about it. I did not want to believe it, but my servants confirmed it."

"But that was at the beginning," said Charlie. "I'll tell you how it was."

He sat down on the hearth and crossed his legs and began to talk quickly, afraid that she might scream for help before she heard it all.

When he had finished, Delphine said quietly, "I am very glad, Charlie, so *very* glad, to hear this. No one told me. Mr. Garnett must have assumed that...that Jules would tell me."

"Then *that's* all right." Charlie grinned. "We looked and looked for you when we got to London, but we couldn't find you no place. The servants at Marsham *wanted* for to tell me, but they couldn't 'cos you'd made them swear they wouldn't. Let's go and see the guv."

"No, Charlie," said Delphine sadly. "Our marriage is over and should never have taken place. I trust you will keep these confidences to yourself."

"You're going to say I'm forgettin' me place," said Charlie, "but I don't care. You never *asks* for explanations when you ought, missus. You saw him kissing and hugging that there Bryce-Connell female, now, didn't you?"

"Yes," said Delphine. "But that is none of your..."

"And you ran away and didn't wait to *see*. That Harriet comes in and walks up to the guv and kisses him on the mouff, and he's that taken aback, he don't know what to do.

"But he pulls back and wipes his mouth and stares at her, oh so haughty, and he says, 'I love my wife, Miss Bryce-Connell, and if I gave you any other impression, I am heartily sorry,' and she ups and offs in a rage."

"Is this true?"

"Of course it's true, and I'd have told him you saw it long ago, only what with all the fighting and all, I didn't get around to it till after Waterloo, and since he followed you up the stairs and come down whistling, I thought it was all right. He told me you had left him an awful note," said Charlie, looking up at Delphine. "He don't talk on familiar terms wiff me as a rule, but it was arter the battle and the social barriers didn't seem that important, I s'pose."

"Oh, dear, I've been such a *fool*!" cried Delphine, clutching her hair.

"Yus," agreed Charlie.

"Where is he now?"

"He's performing as a conjurer at Lady Trowton's party."

"But why...?"

"'Cos we didn't have no money and we couldn't find you, and so he had to make a living same as always. There's a reward coming through for him, but these things take a lot o' time."

"We must go. Now!" said Delphine. "You will take me."

"Wot! Like this?"

"No, of course not. You must have a bath."

"Me! I've never 'ad a bath in all me born days."

"Obviously," said Delphine with a laugh. She rang the bell. Her lady's maid answered promptly, took one look at Charlie, and began to scream the house down.

Servants in various stages of undress came running, Mrs. Castle appeared with a frivolous nightcap over one eye, and the staff had to be quieted and orders given.

At last, by two in the morning, Mrs. Castle and Delphine set off for Lady Trowton's party. Charlie was up on the roof of the coach next to the coachman. He was scrubbed and scented and pomaded.

A page's livery had been found for him. He was still in a state of outrage, and he complained bitterly and incessantly to the coachman that he had been *washed all over*, making a rose-scented bath sound like a rape.

"What is this all about?" Mrs. Castle kept asking.

But Delphine would only shake her head. She did not feel like explaining the long and complicated story of her marriage.

Delphine was wearing an underdress of white crêpe with an overdress of green crêpe, heavily covered with silver spangles. Her hair had been bound tight to her head with a diamond crescent in front and a diamond comb behind. Long diamond earrings blazed in her ears and a magnificent diamond necklace sparkled and shone on her bosom.

Lady Trowton lived in a small townhouse in Great Ormond Street. Delphine had no trouble in gaining admittance, although she did not have an invitation card. Her shining jewels were passport enough.

It appeared that the conjurer was about to give his second performance in a half hour's time. That much Charlie was able to find out from the servants.

Delphine wanted to rush wildly from room to room, searching for him, but Charlie counseled her to be calm.

"It wouldn't be romantic," he said, "to rush into 'is arms wif everybody staring."

Anxious but amused at the same time at Charlie's budding awareness of protocol, Delphine contented herself by strolling from room to room with Mrs. Castle. Charlie, taking his new duties as page seriously, followed her, carrying her fan and stole.

There were fewer people present than Delphine had at first thought. The impression of a larger crowd was given by the many statues which loomed in the candlelight in every room. Marble had been used in profusion, and the gigantic chimneypieces were florid and lavish. Badly painted panels ornamented the walls; figures, putti and medallions, with trophies, swags, and other enrichments, crowded the friezes and panels.

There were many people present whom Delphine had not met, her hostess being one of them.

Delphine exchanged a few polite words with Lady Trowton and thanked her for her "kind invitation," which caused that poor lady much distress, since she could not remember having invited Delphine at all.

Finally, a bell rang, and the butler called to the guests to take their places in the music room for "the entertainment."

Delphine found seats for herself and Mrs. Castle at the back of the room. Charlie stood behind her chair.

"I think it is very strange of Lady Trowton," said a pallid female seated in front of Delphine, "to perpetually want to produce a sort of Astley's Circus. She goes around the street fairs looking for all these oddities."

"Why are we here?" whispered Mrs. Castle for the umpteenth time.

"Very well," murmured Delphine, "I am here to renew acquaintance with my husband."

"What!" screamed Mrs. Castle, and was violently shushed by her neighbors. The show was about to begin.

The first act found favor with the gentlemen but was greeted by silence and haughty stares from the ladies.

A saucy girl with large black eyes and improbable gold hair, with her skirt higher above the ankle than was decent, performed a dance with a gold hoop, leaping nimbly in and out of it like a performing poodle. She sang a song in a thin, little voice, which consisted of a great many tol-rol-diddle-down-days, and was greeted by rapturous applause from the gentlemen of the company.

Next came a gloomy German baritone who sang in his native language with such unmusical force that it sounded like a string of oaths. It all seemed highly cultural, so everyone applauded him in the event it might be thought they didn't understand a word, which was, in fact, the case.

After him, a young man with a prominent Adam's apple recited a long poem he had written himself about the Battle of Waterloo.

Its only literary merit was that the lines eventually rhymed, even if they were not matched in length and were singularly lacking in meter.

> "The cannon roared, the drums they sounded
> and 'What am I to do?'
> Asked Blucher, and Wellington replied,
> 'I don't know, but it's up to me and you.'"

A polite spattering of applause and several groans greeted the end of the epic.

And then the comte strode in front of the audience. Delphine's heart gave a great lurch.

From the top of his guinea-gold curls to his glossy Hessian boots, he looked every inch the English gentleman. His face was as handsome as ever, his blue eyes sleepy and amused.

The pallid woman in front of Delphine sat up. "Isn't he divine!" she breathed.

"That's him, isn't it?" demanded Mrs. Castle, and Delphine nodded.

A table was pushed across the floor next to the comte, containing glasses and cups and plates, which he proceeded to juggle with his usual dexterity. Then he performed a rapid series of conjuring tricks, never once pausing for applause. He produced eggs from ears, scarves from his sleeves, and, finally, two singing canaries from the décolletage of the saucy singer's low-cut gown. This was met by wild applause from everyone, except Delphine, who felt a sharp pang of sheer jealousy.

Then he went back to juggling as the footmen went about the room, putting out the lights.

Just as the last candle was extinguished, the footmen ran on stage carrying blazing torches, which the comte seized from them and proceeded to juggle until he was surrounded by a blazing arc of flame.

The candles were lit again. He deftly caught the torches and doused them in a bucket of water and took his bow.

The crowd of fashionables roared and stamped like children and began to throw money and jewels on the floor at the comte's feet.

"He can't pick them up," said Charlie. "It ain't his place." And with that, he shot forward onto the stage area and began to cheerfully collect everything into a large handkerchief.

The comte winked at Charlie, bowed, and made his exit. Delphine had been twisting a handkerchief in her hands during his performance. It was now in shreds.

Charlie appeared at Delphine's elbow like a jack-in-the-box. "Best takings we ever made," he said cheerfully.

"What did he say when you told him I was here?" asked Delphine.

"Oh, lor'!" Charlie's look of dismay was almost comical. "I was that excited, I forgot."

"Then go and fetch him!" Delphine nearly screamed.

"You must tell me what is going on or I shall *faint!*" wailed Mrs. Castle, but Delphine, with her eyes on Charlie's small, retreating figure, only said, "Later."

"He's gorn," said Charlie dismally when he returned a few moments later.

"Where?"

"Back to those old lodgings of his in Soho. That's one thing about Ma Jenkins, she's that horrible, you can always get a room there when you can't get one anywhere else."

"We must go. Now," said Delphine.

"Well, missus, it might be a better idea if you was to go 'ome and let me fetch him. Can't go running arahnd Soho sparkling like a chandelier," he added, eyeing her jewels.

"No. I am going now, Charlie, and if you won't come, I'm going myself."

"What is happening?" bleated Mrs. Castle pathetically, but Delphine was already on her way out of the door, with Charlie at her heels.

Mrs. Jenkins, the comte's landlady, was leaning against the railings outside her tenement, smoking a foul clay pipe and shaking a squat green bottle to see if there was any gin left in it.

She slowly removed her pipe at the glittering spectacle presented by Delphine.

"They nivir had costooms like those in my day," she said in awe. "I was on the boards, too. *School for Scandal*, I 'member. Full 'ouses, we 'ad."

"You didn't need no school," said Charlie. "W'en it comes to scandal, nobody can teach you."

Charlie jumped back a step as she tried to hit him with her bottle.

Delphine was already on her road up the stairs, feeling her way in the blackness.

"And you can tell that doxy," came Mrs. Jenkins's unlovely voice, "that I keeps a 'spectable 'ouse."

"Garn!" came Charlie's answer. "Every strolling mort in London's got a lay here."

There came the sounds of an undignified scuffle. Mrs. Castle had remained in the coach and was now cowering in the far corner of the carriage seat, wondering if they would all get out alive.

"Jules!" called Delphine into the blackness of the staircase. She could not remember which room she had been in before. She did not even know whether he would be in the same room, even supposing she could remember where it was.

"Jules!" she called more loudly.

Various angry voices told her to "stow it." A door opened, and a villainous-looking old man looked down at her.

And then, all at once, the comte was there, holding up a candle and leaning over the bannister.

Delphine ran wildly up the stairs towards him. She threw herself against his chest, crying, "Come home with me, Jules. I love you."

"Quietly," he said, drawing her inside the room.

Before he closed the door, a loud chorus from the other inhabitants serenaded them with various lewd suggestions as to what they could do with themselves.

The comte placed the candle on a rickety table beside the bed and turned and held out his arms.

She walked straight into them and turned her face up for his kiss.

But he held her a little away from him. "I am not going to make love to you here," he said quietly. "I have missed you so dreadfully."

"I thought you and Harriet..."

"I know. Charlie told me, finally. We've wasted so much time."

"There is so much you must tell me," said Delphine. "What happened to that Frenchman? The spy."

"Dead. He broke his neck trying to escape his prison. Isn't there something else you wish me to tell you?"

162

Delphine looked at him in mute appeal.

"I love you, my heart," he said. "I never told you that."

"I love you, too," said Delphine.

He kissed her suddenly and fiercely, feeling her body melt into his.

"Oh, Jules," murmured Delphine when she could. "It is time to go home."

"To Marsham?"

"Yes."

"And will you take this poor mountebank as he is? I cannot be another Sir George."

"I would not wish you any other way," said Delphine softly. "Come."

"Wait a bit," he said, turning at the door. "I am forgetting my hard-earned winnings. You know, my heart, I was well on the way to making a fortune!"

"Oh, *Jules*," Delphine sighed. She had been about to add, "Will you never change?" but realized just in time that she never wanted him to be anything other than what he was at that moment.

Maria Bencastle learned of the couple's return to Marsham Manor and decided to pay them a visit to see if she could ingratiate herself into Delphine's good graces.

She had found herself a small house on the outskirts of Hegsley. But it was a lonely mode of existence. It was the very breath of life to Maria to interfere in someone else's business. She could not bear living alone.

She accordingly pasted a humble smile on her heavy features as Bradley answered the door of Marsham Manor.

"I am afraid his lordship and her ladyship are abed," said the butler.

Maria's eyes flew past him to the clock in the hall. "But it is two in the afternoon!" she exclaimed.

Bradley gave an irritatingly Gallic shrug. "Milord needs his rest." He smirked.

"That man," said Maria, turning on her heel, "is bone lazy!"

Upstairs, in milord's tumbled bed, Delphine turned her head and looked at him.

"My love," she ventured, "it is time to consider the wages for the itinerant harvest workers. Perhaps if we..."

"No," he interrupted. "I can't be bothered. Garnett will see to it."

"You are bone lazy!" protested Delphine, unknowingly echoing Maria. "Don't you have energy for anything?"

He pulled her into his arms. "The only exertion I enjoy, my heart, is...*this*."

"Oh, Jules." Delphine sighed, happily surrendering herself to the inevitable.

"*What* a convenient marriage!"